MARYSE MEIJER RAG

LEWIS McVEY

Maryse Meijer is the author of the story collection *Heartbreaker*, which was one of Electric Literature's 25 Best Short Story Collections of 2016, and the novella *Northwood*. She lives in Chicago.

ALSO BY MARYSE MEIJER

Heartbreaker: Stories
Northwood: A Novella

RAG

Rag

STORIES

Maryse Meijer

FSG Originals | FARRAR, STRAUS AND GIROUX *New York*

Meijer

FSG Originals
Farrar, Straus and Giroux
175 Varick Street, New York 10014

Grateful acknowledgment is made to the following publications, in
which these stories originally appeared, in slightly different form:
Paper Darts ("Rag," "Good Girls"); *The Adroit Journal* ("The
Brother"); *The Collagist* ("Evidence"); *Washington Square Review*
("The Lover"); *Indiana Review* ("Alice"); *Exit 7* ("Francis"); *The
Conium Review* ("Her Blood"); and *Slush Pile Magazine* ("At the Sea").

Library of Congress Cataloging-in-Publication Data
Names: Meijer, Maryse, 1982– author.
Title: Rag : stories / Maryse Meijer.
Description: First edition. | New York : Farrar, Straus and Giroux,
    2019.
Identifiers: LCCN 2018034446 | ISBN 9780374246235 (pbk.)
Classification: LCC PS3613.E4264 A6 2019 | DDC 813/.6—dc23
LC record available at https://lccn.loc.gov/2018034446

Designed by Richard Oriolo

FOR DANIELLE

CONTENTS

RAG

HER BLOOD

EXCUSE ME? she said. Help, I need—can you help me?

She was standing at the side of the counter, in the hall-way that led to the booths and the bathroom. Blood pasting her white jeans to her thighs. She was hunched almost double, arms wrapped around her stomach, limp hair lashing her face. She smiled around a crop of buck teeth. A strand of saliva looped to the floor. Sorry, she said, wiping her mouth on her wrist. I'm sorry.

Are you okay? I asked, stepping backward, away from her, until my foot met the wall. The smell of burning sausage poured from the ovens.

I had a miscarriage, she said. In your bathroom?

I opened my mouth, imagining an actual baby in there, slick and twisting on the tile.

Maybe you could call someone? she suggested, her voice very small, high, like a child's. Blood all the way to her socks. An ambulance?

Okay, I said, reaching for the wall phone, okay—

I turned the OPEN sign off and sat beside her in a booth. I kept thinking how the splits in the vinyl bench would soak up the stuff coming out of her. Jason would be pissed, like I'd spilled my own blood there on purpose. The girl trembled, knees tight together, making a sound like *hm, hm*, as her hands, thin but veined like a man's, crept over her elbows. I didn't think to put down a towel or give her a glass of water. She leaned over the tabletop to look out the window, neon from the shop signs pooling in the flooded gutters.

Do you think they're coming soon? she asked. Even her hair had blood in it, from where she'd sat on it, or pushed it back with her fingers. I moved away, to the very edge of the seat, and she whispered, calmly, still facing the window, It's okay.

When the ambulance stopped at the curb I could see two men, heads down in the rain, carrying a stretcher. Oh, she said, and then the men were in the room, dripping onto the mats, and I stood up so they could touch her wrist and flash lights in her face. When they asked her What happened her eyes slid over to mine and she smiled, sucking her lower lip between those enormous teeth, before passing out in their arms.

I spent an hour in the bathroom with a bucket of bleach and paper towels and a pair of yellow gloves with crud in the fingertips. I wiped the porcelain over and over with one hand while I breathed into my elbow. There was something the size of a steak in the toilet, sunk in the red water, organ-like; it didn't look like a baby, but maybe there was a piece of a baby inside—an eye, a finger, a face—and I wondered if there was something I should do with it, but I couldn't think of anything. I flushed, coughing. The thing squeezed down the pipe, and little bits of whatever it was gurgled back up into the pit of the bowl so that I had to stand there and flush until the water was clear.

She'd used up the toilet paper, stuffed long red ropes of it into the trash. There were meat-colored streaks all over the floor where she'd walked in her own blood. And the graffiti on the walls that Jason loved—that's what she had to look at while it happened, things like *Wesley King eats dick* and *Fuck off and die*. The overhead light was dim and the dark blue walls were almost black and I knew I wasn't seeing it all, getting it all, the mess she'd made, but I couldn't stand it anymore, so I left. I took the trash out to the dumpsters and ate cold pepperoni and drank a cup of Mountain Dew. The phone rang.

Hi, she said. Hi, it's you?

I spit the pepperoni into a napkin. Yes, how—

I'm sorry, she said, I know—there was a mess. I would have cleaned it. I would have—

It's fine, I interrupted. I could still feel the pepperoni in my mouth, slippery, rancid. Are you okay?

Oh, yes, she said. Yes.

That's good, I said.

Thank you, you know, for—calling the ambulance. For staying with me.

It's fine. There was a long pause; when she spoke again her voice was whispery but loud at the same time, like she had her mouth pressed up against the receiver.

Did you see it? she asked.

See what?

When you were cleaning up, she said. Did you see anything?

I thought of the black shape in the water, its gleaming sides.

Not really, I said.

I did, she said, sniffing. I touched it, even. I thought it would be, you know, that you could see what it looked like. But it wasn't a baby. It was something else.

Her voice broke off. A little breath.

And you—you just—flushed it, right? she said.

Yeah, I—I mean, you left it there, I—

She giggled. No, I mean, of course, it's okay, that's great, you were really great, she said, and she stayed on the line for a moment, and so did I, listening to her, listening to her listening to me, and then she made a noise, like a part of a laugh, or a sob, and then she hung up.

I walked home in the rain, up to my ankles in the filthy water. It was a Monday night and everything was closed. I wondered if they'd given her new clothes to wear at the hospital, or if someone'd brought her something to change into—I didn't know how it all worked, who would clean her, how she would clean herself. There'd been a trail of blood from the bathroom to the counter to the booth to the door, blood on the medics' blue suits as they carried her out. I imagined having what she had, a place in my body that could splash an entire room with my insides and then let me walk away. I got an erection though I didn't mean to. I pushed my hands into the front pocket of my hoodie and rubbed them against my crotch, grimacing, not feeling good at all. When I got to my apartment my roommates were already in bed and I fell on the couch in my wet clothes and went to sleep.

The next time I saw her she wasn't alone. Her boyfriend towered over her, with a thick red beard and a gut of hard fat stacked over the belt of his khakis. She was pressed against his side, her head grazing his armpit, in a tank top and a short corduroy skirt, showing off her flat chest and pale legs. He ordered a slice of the Five Meat and she wanted a Diet Coke. He took their change and I gave her a cup. Our fingers touched. I turned to get some crusts from the freezer, feeling her gaze crawl up my neck; when I glanced back at her she was smiling. I went around the ovens to the sink just to get away from them. He said something and she laughed. I stared at the rack of dirty pans and counted the days since she'd come in, two, three, four—why was she laughing? How long did you have to wait until you could laugh again after something like that? Finally I heard the door open and I walked to the front. She had her head on his arm, her hair grazing her waist. I looked for the blood but of course it wasn't there. Bye, she said, and I said Bye, out of habit, back.

They came in once or twice a week, sitting in the booth where we'd sat together, her ass or his ass right on top of the tape I'd put over the split in the seat, right on top of where her blood had been, still was. I knew they were fucking a lot. He would grab her bony wrists and pull her across the table for a kiss, her body jerking like a puppet, and while he ate he grinned at her like he was thinking about something dirty. If he was on top of her—I imagined it against my will. How could it not hurt her? He was so big. That sloppy body, his filthy beard. I was nineteen. I was a virgin. The counter came all the way up to her chest and when they ordered she stood there kneading the edge of it with her thumbs in this weird way. I didn't know what to do. I served her, I served her boyfriend. I cleaned up after them—their dirty plates, their crushed napkins—I let them smear themselves all over the place. She had a habit of putting her forehead right on the window when she looked out of it. The grease from her face left a mark on the glass and I wiped that off, too.

I peed into a Styrofoam cup on my breaks. During the shift overlap I watched the others tick off their names on the bathroom maintenance clipboard but I didn't tick mine. Jason came in at the end of my shift and started saying he couldn't trust me if I slacked off whenever he went out of town. I stood against the wall and nodded, keeping myself very still. He went to take a piss. I waited. What the fuck, he shouted a minute later, the door banging against the wall as he kicked the plunger into the hallway. The toilet's fucking clogged, he said. I didn't move. He snapped his fingers in my face. Hey. Genius. Wake up. I said I'd take care of it. I don't remember if I did. I don't remember ever going back in that bathroom again.

But she did. Both of them did. Once they went in there together and when they came out she was licking her lips and giggling. When she saw me looking she stopped. A muscle in her cheek twitched and her lips were struggling to get around her buck teeth. I kept staring at her. Her boyfriend was leaning over the stack of flyers beneath the window, his foot in the air, and she was caught between the two of us, between me and him, me and the black door behind her.

You're there, good, you're there, she said, and it was like the time she called from the hospital or wherever; she was out of breath, her mouth right up to the phone.

It's late, she said, I can't believe you work so late.

You're up, I pointed out.

Oh, well, I'm always up, she said.

What about your boyfriend?

My boyfriend?

The guy you're with.

You mean Dennis, that's Dennis. Her *s*'s hissed a little, like a lisp. He's not here.

I wondered what that meant. If they lived together, if he was out somewhere without her and that's why she was calling me, or if there was some other reason, one I couldn't guess.

Does he know? I asked, swallowing.

About . . . ?

About what . . . happened.

She paused, like she didn't know what I meant. Oh, she said eventually, no. I mean, not really.

Oh, I echoed.

I used to come in a lot, she said, tentative, almost a question. Before. By myself?

You did?

Don't you remember?

No—

I work near you. I mean I saw you so many times.

I was sure I would have recognized her. Someone who looked like her. I had a feeling she was lying. I didn't say anything, just dug my finger beneath a broken flap of plastic on the register drawer.

He didn't know that I'd been already, she said. He thought it was his idea. To go there. He likes your pizza.

It's not my pizza. It comes frozen.

Well, he likes it. Do you mind? I mean, that we come in so much? That I'm calling? You must be busy, she said. You're always by yourself.

It's fine, I said. You work down here, too? Where?

She paused. Just down the street, she answered. Not far at all.

Where do you live?

Not far, she repeated.

I broke open a sleeve of Styrofoam cups with one hand. Why are you calling? I mean, do you want something?

No, she said. I just thought—

Never mind, I said, stacking the cups next to the register. I thought about the way she'd sat in the booth, making that sound, the raw smell of her so strong I had to breathe through my mouth. I pushed the cups into line with my finger. There was a dustless circle where they always stood and I had to get them into that circle. Water was sliding down the front window in thick ropes and I flexed my toes in my shoes, still wet from the night before. It would not stop raining.

I let myself imagine this was some kind of game for them, a routine: he'd fuck her and she'd get pregnant and then she'd take something, medicine or something, and they'd wait for the thing to happen. He'd send her into these places to do it, and he'd meet her at the hospital and she'd tell him who had touched her and what it felt like and he'd fuck her again as soon as they got home, and there'd be a pile somewhere, of her jeans, stiff, rust-colored, that she would never wash or throw away. The smell of stale blood filling their bedroom and the fact of her pain just that, a fact, and not something that could really hurt her, because she'd been scraped out so often that everything breakable had already been broken and cleared away. She would be smooth inside, as smooth and slick as wet rock. There was something so fucked up about them, about her, the way she smiled at me with her boyfriend standing right there, as if we'd met at a party, as if we were friends, as if what had happened had never really happened at all.

I didn't have an umbrella and I never got one. Jason said it was monsoon season and I thought that was a real thing until I looked it up online and saw that it was only for India. I used that joke with her the next time they came in. Dennis leaned against the counter and said Goddamn rain, right man? And I said Yeah, it's like a fucking monsoon out there, and she seemed pleased, snorting with her mouth open. I slung his pizza onto a paper plate and didn't charge her for her soda. He clapped my shoulder and said You're a good guy. She wrapped her arms around his bicep and beamed. They'd tracked in a lot of mud and while they ate I got the mop and cleaned the floor, swabbing beneath their table so they had to raise their feet before settling them back, still filthy, onto the damp tile.

. . .

She always called at the same time, after we'd closed, when I was cleaning up. I didn't say Hello, Party Pizza when I answered, just waited for her to talk. There was this moment, when we both were listening to each other, breathing, that made me feel like I was turning into smoke, expanding, filling the room, and she was there, filling it with me. Then she'd say Hey, it's me, in her tiny voice. I didn't know her name. I still don't.

Do you have friends? she asked me that night. A lot of friends?

I tucked the phone against my shoulder, counting money from the drawer.

I have roommates, I said. Two.

Boys?

Yeah.

Are they home when you get home?

What?

I'm sorry, she said, I just—thought of you as going home by yourself.

They go out a lot. It's mostly just me.

Oh. I never lived with other girls, she said. I went right from home to being with Dennis. We met at a concert. I was dancing and someone hit me on my cheek, by accident, and I had a cut and Dennis helped me fix it up.

I could hear her smiling. I imagined her holding her hand to her face, lost in a crowd, letting people slam into her. I imagined being there, standing against the wall. I'd see her get hit and I wouldn't help her. I would just watch the wound open up and she'd see me watching, she'd let the blood run down her shirt. It's not that I wanted to see her get hurt. I hated everything about what had happened to her. But that sound she made, her smallness, the way she showed herself to me—that's what I saw, what I still wanted to see.

When the phone rang the next night I picked up but it wasn't her; it was him, breathing hard.

Hey, he said. It's Dennis. She there?

We're closed, I said.

Right, right, shit, he said, with a little laugh. Shit, man. Sorry. Yeah.

Is she—

It's cool, it's cool, she'll be back any minute. I just thought she said she was going to get some food and that was a while ago, so you know. Just thought I'd call 'cause she left her phone here so I can't get ahold of her.

We close at ten, I said.

Yeah, okay man, see you later then, he said, and hung up, still panting. I squeezed myself through my jeans, my head against the wall. After a moment I opened one eye and there she was, at the window, watching me, her hands cupped against the glass.

The next time they came in she looked at me with her eyebrows high, like we had a secret, but we always had a secret, or they did, or I did—I didn't know who knew what or what there was to know. I wasn't charging them for drinks and Dennis went back for refills twice. I thought maybe he'd gained weight. She had her feet on top of his under the table and was making little rips in the scalloped edge of his paper plate. When they left Dennis turned and gave me the thumbs-up and I smiled like I knew what that meant.

Was it your first time?

She giggled. My first time what?

Having, you know—it happen.

I could hear her shifting, her body rubbing against something, I wondered if her hair was in her face, like it always was when I saw her, or if it was pulled back, and, if so, what her face was like when it was bare, if there was something behind all that hair that she was hiding.

I didn't even know that I was pregnant. I thought I was dying, she said. I really did.

Uh, I said.

Was it your first time, too?

I blinked. What?

Seeing that. A girl like that.

Y-yeah, I said. Obviously. Yes.

It's not that uncommon, she said. The doctor said it happens all the time. Not to the same person, I mean, just in general. Sometimes you don't even know what it is, you think it's just cramps or a weird period or something. But mine was . . . farther along.

She took a deep breath, then sighed. I know what you think, she said. You think I'd just leave you alone. You think I'd—do something different. She paused. But I do this instead. I can't help it. I love it, she said in that breathless whisper, and I was suddenly so hard it hurt.

Why?

I don't know! she exclaimed in wonder. The way you look at me. Do you know how you do it? Is it something you do on purpose?

What?

Like—like you hate me, she said, swallowing. Like you can't stop.

I don't hate you.

Oh, it doesn't matter. Maybe there's a different word for it. For that way you look.

I wiped the counter with a paper towel, in a circle, the same circle over and over.

Did it hurt a lot?

Yes, she said.

I was quiet. The counter was cleaner than it had ever been and yet it still felt sticky.

Do you want children? she whispered.

No.

You're lucky, she said, her voice thinning out, a wisp, floating away from me.

Come here, I said, squeezing the phone in my sweaty hand. Come alone.

She exhaled—not surprised, not unhappy—and for a moment I thought I had a chance, the future bloomed out before me, and then she said He's home, and hung up.

GOOD GIRLS

I WOKE up and smelled them and followed their smell—

—shampoo perfume sweat lotion cheap clothes conditioner
nail polish blood—

—to the house with its broken screens and the cracked
kitchen glass and the holes in between the boards and
its skinny walls—their bodies flashing endlessly in the
windows—

—they had long blond hair I found it everywhere—on the
porch or in the yard or on the sidewalks or buried in
the grass—I rolled in it and it stuck to me—

. . .

—it better not shit on the lawn one of them said—that was the first thing they said about me when they saw me squatting near the front door—I didn't shit but I did piss on the grass when they weren't looking—

—there was a woman in the house—not the mother—she would say about the slamming doors or the radio on too loud or some other thing *girls!!!*—but the girls didn't care—

—I think the mother was dead and the father too—

—dude it's like it's obsessed with us—does it have tags? one of them wanted to know grabbing me by the neck—*look idiot it doesn't even have a collar it's obviously homeless— what kind is it—it looks like a Shepherd* one of them said—*no those are bigger maybe a Boxer* said another—*what the hell are you talking about if you think that's a purebred you're out of your fucking mind—*

—I remembered being a man what it was like walking on two legs and having arms to put around a girl's shoulders and the way her bones felt if you squeezed her—I remembered sitting up at a table and eating with a fork—but I didn't remember my name or how long I had lived or when I stopped being a man exactly—so I can't say if I miss it—

. . .

—I breathed against the house at night—sometimes they were sleeping sometimes they were whispering into the phone—sometimes they were crying in the beds or in the bathroom—I smelled their wet faces and their lips against the receivers and their feet rubbing together beneath their dirty sheets—

—it had been a long time since I'd been a body in that kind of bed—alone and with other bodies—whose names I can't remember and maybe never knew—

—none of them liked to get up in the morning they had to be pounced on or bitten or smacked on the butt by whoever turned the alarm off—

—they microwaved bacon and wiped their greasy hands on the chair cushions—they tried to make eggs but burned them every time—going out of the room and then coming back to a blackened pan—they ate cold pastry from foil packets or peanut butter fingered from a jar—sometimes they gave me chips or let me lap up the crumbs they left behind as they walked—

—they loved to call each other names or punch each other's arms or pull each other's hair—often I saw just a tangle of bodies in the house the girls so close together on the couch or sharing a bed and trying to get a signal on the cell phone they found in the street—they were always finding things or hiding things or taking things home—and some of these things I remembered the name for and some of them I recognized but could not name—like when one of the girls had a bag in her hand—clutching it by its neck she whispered to another girl *don't tell* and then she dumped the bag over the bed and out came a pile of black lace—and they smiled just looking at the black things and smearing them around on the blanket and giggling—

—I got into the house once when the woman left the back door open—I ran in and I headed straight for the place where the black things were and I took one and buried it in their yard beneath a bush so I could sniff it and always know where it was—

—they had parties—they put Christmas lights on the back porch and mixed alcohol in a bucket—some friends came—four boys in a truck—I showed my teeth and fear popped through their flesh and the girls wrapped their heads around the side of the house and yelled DON'T WORRY HE'S FRIENDLY—

—the one place it was hard to see in was the bathroom when they were in the shower because the steam clogged the window and I shoved my eye against the glass again and again legs trembling I sniffed as hard as I could—smell of hot flesh and soap—*girls!* the woman yelled inside—*how many times do I have to tell you no dirty pant-ies in the sink!*—

—which is what they wore lying in the backyard on a blanket—I came running I drooled over their brown knees—they hit me on the head but I kept on doing it—until they sprayed me with the hose—

—they were doing that thing where it was a school night and they weren't going anywhere but they acted like they were—a red shirt thrown over the lamp and the girls draw-ing on their faces and grabbing things out of each other's hands and bending to look at themselves in the dresser mirror—their jeans so tight their hips puffed out over the top—one of them took a bottle and shook it over her arms—liquid crawling from elbow to wrist—someone put on the radio and they stepped on the bed and closed their eyes—fake fruit smell—the other girls said *oh god it stinks!*—and the girl at the mirror said *it's designer!*—and they screamed back *it still stinks!!!!!!*

—but everything smelled good to me—

—they walked to their school together carrying books one of them always running to catch up one of them always combing her hair one of them always looking into the cars that passed all of them always talking at the same time—*it's following us again—I think he's cute—ugh are you kid-ding he's got mange—I think he belonged to the guy with the trailer in the backyard but got away—oh you mean the guy who did all those drugs and blew up his grandma's garage— yeah him—I heard he was in jail—I heard he was dead—I heard he beat all his kids and they still wanted to live in that shithole—why do you think anyone does meth if they know it's going to fuck up their face with scabs and shit I mean crack makes more sense just like cosmetically—shh there's Mr. Kinkaid—where—in the car—oh my god don't smile at him*—but they did smile at him it was like an itch they had their mouths moving whenever they saw a boy or a man and when the car pulled into the parking lot I pissed on its tires—

—I was made for finding meat and eating it—how natural it came to me—a rat in my mouth they saw me at night a light pointed at me they screamed *ew DISGUSTING!!*— I dropped the rat—and left it but still they wouldn't let me lick them for a week—

—they whispered *we should call the cops on you they'd put you in the pound they'd euthanize you*—grinning as they said it—but when I whined they said *oh for fuck's sake don't be so pathetic*—and slammed the door as they went inside and the woman said—*why do you let that dirty thing follow you around*—and the girls snapped back *we DON'T it just DOES—*

—they were no longer in school and the house throbbed with the smell of them even the jasmine even the barbecues even the new tar on the roads was crushed beneath their smell they gathered in the backyard and one of them was smiling to herself the others pushed her shoulders saying *what is it—what—*

—when finally from out of her pocket she pulled the thing and held it in her lap for them to see—*oh my god give it to me you don't even know how to work it—don't point it at me!!!—I'm not I'm just showing you—it looks real—it is real—I mean no like it could kill someone—well you could if you got them in just the right place* another one said— *what's the right place?—right HERE* one of them said and pushed the other's head—I was in the bush on the other side of their driveway next to the neighbor's fence and they said *come! come out! come here!* slapping their thighs— *sit! stay!* they giggled and one of them pushed on my butt and my legs buckled beneath me the ground very hot against my belly—I rolled on my side and they pushed their shoes against my ribs—they cooed in a long loopy song as they dropped potato chips on my face—and poured soda over my head which stung when it got in my eyes and made a pool beneath me sticky and spreading—they ate the rest of the chips and one of them was mad about not having any more orange soda—*you do it—no you no YOU!!!*—they fumbled the stuff between them and the empty bag was tossed on the lawn—they stopped giggling their bodies throwing shadows over mine and I tried to get them all in my eye at the same time—they had a whole sack of the metal balls and they emptied them into me the mouth of that thing against my mouth against my ribs on my tail one by one taking turns I just lay there and whined—*it's not a lot of blood at all—it's just a BB gun what did you expect*—they were grabbing it out of each other's hands—arguing—one of them put one of the balls in the other's arm click click—the girl who was shot screamed so loud I couldn't hear anything for many long moments—*shit you cunts!!!* she shouted bent in half her hair hanging down almost touching me I moved my leg and she groaned—they had been drinking vodka—she vomited and then they were all laughing again sitting on the ground and falling over each other they forgot about the thing and the pellets and her puffy arm with its little red eye of wound—clutching their stomachs their legs a heap kicking the ground they were helpless helplessly happy—*what the fuck!!!!!!!*—laughing—laughter—

—I licked their hands I was shivering all over they tasted like salt and like the way they smelled I could barely breathe and I sank into the middle of them I was bleeding a little from a lot of different places and they laughed and laughed at me but I didn't mind—

—I'd had my chance as a man.

ALICE

FRIDAY NIGHTS used to be Steak Nights. Exactly ten ounces of prime rib for me, eight for Wendy, six for our daughter Alice. Other nights we had fish and green vegetables, tofu and brown rice; but Friday was about flesh and blood.

Then a Friday came and there was only one steak at the table, set at Alice's place. I drank my milk, stared at my empty plate. It was Alice's twelfth birthday. After that Alice ate meat every day, and Wendy never served me meat again.

We didn't say that Alice was getting fat. She was. She was getting very fat. She grew hips, a double chin, several extra stomachs. Alice's teachers sent home notes and made phone calls, but Wendy handled those. She used the word *thyroid* a lot. Wendy prepared all the meals. I wasn't allowed to give Alice snacks or treats of any kind. I did the shopping at the natural foods market; I bought the steaks in bulk from the butcher. He thought we were giving them to our dogs. We didn't have dogs. Just a daughter.

Wendy panfried the steaks until they were barely warm. No matter how much deodorizer she sprayed, the house always smelled like blood. We weren't allowed to help in the kitchen; we weren't allowed to open the refrigerator. The only exception was when I did the grocery shopping and put away the food. There were slots for everything: Greek yogurt, vegetables, milk. Nothing touched anything else. The meat was triple-wrapped. Poor meat. I poked a hole in the cellophane and the meat dripped on the glass shelf. Are you sad? I asked it. It dripped some more. I gave the steak a kiss and it was a lot like other kisses I'd had: cold, smooth, dead. And yet this meat would feed a living person, the person I loved most, it would help make so much more of her. I kissed it again, out of gratitude, and the kiss sank into the meat, becoming a vitamin, a protein, fuel, ready to hit the pan screaming.

I hadn't worked since Alice was born. I washed the dishes, did the cleaning, completed the list of chores Wendy left for me each morning. On my lunch breaks I drove to Alice's school and sat in my car, eating Wendy's tiny sushi rolls and miso soups and drinking cold green tea. I didn't taste any of it. It was like eating air. From the street I could see right through the window of Alice's English class. Her head was like a ball balanced perfectly atop a larger ball, so elegant, so very beautiful that I could never believe, from a distance, that she was mine, something from my own body. Her dark hair always clean, gleaming. She had a pencil box I had given her many years before, yellow with blue and red dots, which she held in her lap; I think Wendy put strips of beef jerky in it. When the bell rang and Alice went off to History I rolled up my lunch bag and put my seat back and fell asleep.

One afternoon I found a ten-dollar bill wadded up in the gutter skirting our front lawn. I hadn't seen unbudgeted money in years. I drove to a fast-food restaurant and ordered three hamburgers and ate them all during Alice's class, sucking the grease from my fingers for a long time. The taste of fat, that's what grease is. We all love to put it inside ourselves, even Wendy, Wendy loves it and that's why she won't eat it. Wendy has a hard time with love.

I put the bag under the seat, thinking I would throw it away in the neighbor's trash when I got home, but I forgot. Wendy found it.

This, she said, shoving the bag in my face. This is disgusting.

It was after dinner. Alice was in bed. I was scrubbing the sink with a toothbrush. I took a deep breath.

Wendy, you give Alice meat every—

I give her *steak*, not *garbage*, Wendy hissed. Alice is *growing*. Alice has a *condition*.

I blinked. What condition?

Don't be ignorant. I could smell this from the driveway. You bring this poison into our house?

I didn't bring it inside.

It's inside your body, which is inside our house, she said, throwing the bag out onto the back porch. I followed it. She tossed a box of laxatives at my feet. How her nostrils flared when she was angry, a vein pulsing beneath the skin. She was probably pretty, most likely very pretty, but it had been a long time since I'd seen her prettiness. I imagined kissing her, or grabbing her by the hair. I didn't want to do either. I smiled. After a moment she slammed the door.

I stayed in the guesthouse for two days, taking the laxatives. Nobody had ever stayed in the guesthouse except me and it was, like the main house, pristine. I plumped the decorative pillows on the bed and kept my shoes off the comforter when I watched TV. Alice brought me water and green tea and fruit, lingering on the doorstep while I ate an apple.

Did you really have three hamburgers? she asked, glancing at me.

Wendy told you?

She's still really mad.

I know. I shouldn't have done it.

Alice pushed her thumb against the doorjamb, rubbing the smooth white paint. Do you miss it? she asked, tipping her head to the side, her neck folding in smooth rolls over the collar of her dress.

Meat?

She nodded.

No, I answered. Not anymore. I've had plenty in my life, I said. It's for you, now.

Alice smiled. How's the apple?

Good. I chewed, swallowed. Crisp, I added.

Isn't there anything you miss?

I thought. Maybe ice cream.

Alice's eyes widened. You used to eat ice cream?

I think so, I said. It was a long time ago. Before you were born.

She touched my stomach then, very lightly, looking at me to see if it was okay. I still had some muscle there. Wendy liked to say that what we ate made us what we were; Wendy wanted to be something like a rock garden, pure, hard, blameless. What did she want our daughter to be? Giving her all that gristle, all that fat. But fat is pure, too. So white and solid. Wendy wouldn't have thought of that.

What did you have for breakfast? I asked.

Bacon, Alice said. And a Polish sausage.

And lunch?

A ham sandwich.

Good, I said. Good girl.

I gave her the core of the apple and she closed her hand around it like it was something precious. I couldn't remember the last time she'd had fruit.

What's your mother doing now?

She's vacuuming.

Do you want to come in?

Alice nodded. I sat on the couch.

Come here, I said, patting my knee. I was not invited to Alice's doctor's visits. I didn't know what she weighed. The last time I knew her numbers she was a month old and weighed less than a week's worth of prime rib.

Oof, I said when she sat down. Her flesh hung down all around my thighs, bumped my stomach, filled my arms. I hugged her waist. My legs went numb almost instantly.

Am I big? she asked, looking down at me.

You are very big.

Am I pretty?

You are very pretty.

She blushed. We sat like that for a moment, in silence. Part of me wanted to eat what she ate, to share in her pleasure at the table, to join her wherever she was going; but I knew that part of raising a child is to set them on a path that isn't yours. I was turning into air; that was natural. But she, she would have what she deserved. Nothing could dislodge her from the earth; she would stick to it and everything would stick to her: experiences, life, joy. Her body was making room for it all, each cell exceeding its limits. She was growing up.

Good? I said after a moment. She smiled.

Good.

I came back to the main house. Fish was now off the menu; yogurt, cheese, and milk followed suit. The refrigerator was nearly free of food, filled instead with a cool violet light. The butcher was ordering meat from a small organic farm outside our suburb; it came in a crate and cost a fortune. Alice grew and grew. Her skin was very clear and her teeth were perfect. She smelled wonderful. We were careful not to let Wendy see us when Alice sat on my lap. Wendy didn't know what was pure and what wasn't; we went along with her way of doing things, but for our own reasons. Wendy appeared on a workout video for vegans and when I saw my wife's sweatless face looking into the camera with such rigid determination I laughed. At dinner I ate my spoonful of rice and when I caught Alice's eye she smiled, her cheeks full of meat.

I spent more and more time parked outside the school. I didn't bother with Wendy's lunches; I put them straight in the trash. Those burgers had cured me. I was never hungry anymore. I slipped in and out of sleep while I waited for Alice. Summer was coming. Such blue skies. And Alice through the window, pulling something from her pencil box. Something raw. Liver? Chicken? She chewed and wrote in her notebook, swallowed and raised her hand to answer a question. I put my cheek on the passenger seat and fell asleep again.

That evening, while Wendy did the dishes, I took Alice on my lap and felt how much heavier she had become since the day before. I was speechless. How did she do it? My knee trembled. She giggled.

I don't know what's wrong with her, Wendy said that

night, looking at herself in the bathroom mirror. There's no fat gene in my family.

Hm, I said.

You don't seem concerned.

I think she's fine, I said.

You always think that, she said darkly, snapping a piece of floss from its box. I shrugged and stood on the scale. Double digits. I smiled.

What? she said. I blocked the number with my foot.

Nothing, I said.

I dreamt about living on pills, a glass of protein powder. I woke up choking, spitting blood on the pillow, the blood making the shapes of everything I'd ever craved: french fries, apple pies, barbecue. I beheld them with delight, no trace of hunger, my stomach a vat of calm, happy acid. Wendy's gold head right next to mine, still asleep. I took the pillow, held it above her face, but didn't press down.

I drove to Alice's school that afternoon, even though it was a Saturday. Wendy was with Alice at the doctor's office, testing her blood for the third time that month. I closed my mouth around the stale air of the car; what would be floating there? Pieces of skin, particles of plastic, flakes of leather from the tan seats, all the dust of this particular moment. I closed my eyes and semen pumped effortlessly from my penis; the last of that liquid. I opened my eyes; there in the dark window of the classroom I saw Alice, standing with her pencil box in one hand, waving with the other. I waved back.

At dinner I pushed my food away, silverware untouched, the minute scoop of rice and kale pristine on the plate. Wendy shook with rage. How dare I eat less than her, she was thinking. How dare it be so easy for me to refuse what she still needed. She told me I was ill, that Alice was ill, that she, Wendy, was trying her best to keep the family healthy but we never helped her. She stood at the head of the table, pointing her fork at my face. I could see a lot of veins beneath the skin of her arms, pulsing a livid blue. Hate, I knew, was keeping her alive. Her hate was in the food and that's why I didn't need it. But I'd kissed the meat that morning; I kissed it every morning. I turned Wendy's hate into love.

You're a sick bastard, Wendy said.

I turned my face toward the smell of cooling beef. Alice was sitting very still, her knife frozen above her plate, watching us. There just wasn't enough for everyone. I don't know why.

I took my daughter's hand. Honey, I said, finish your food.

POOL

JACOB SAW the splash and the body going down. Slow motion. The girls' screams, sun, the red cement, everyone crawling over the side of the pool. He swam like a motherfucker to the deep end, panting as he flipped the body over, a sheet of blood over the face, a man's face, mouth open and reeking chlorine. A tooth missing. A tooth way down in the water. A swollen eye and a huge wound weeping above it, bone winking between gaping lips of skin. With the help of two other junior guards Jacob hauled the body out. His mouth eventually on the body's mouth. His hands pressing the chest. Blood and air, blood and air, Jacob bent above the body and then finally Mr. Long shoving him aside, a siren slicing through the sudden silence, the girls huddled against the fence, and the boys dripping in a circle around the body and the pool turning to glass beneath the summer sun.

Jacob stands at the sink, hot water running and running. It had been over in a second. The body taken away. The waistband of Jacob's swim trunks the same color as the stains on the cement outside. The blood had run from head to chest, tongue to stomach, mouth to mouth. He puts his face to the glass and his breath turns to smoke. Keep breathing, he thinks. Keep breathing.

Bobby is the name of the body and Bobby is fine. Stitches and a concussion and the lost tooth and shaken up but fine, back at school three days after the accident, walking the hall thinking Is it him or him or him? Imagining a football-type, a senior, though Long had said You know, the skinny blond, my best swimmer. All he has to do is ask someone to point the kid out but he won't do that, he doesn't want anyone to know he cares, that he's thinking about it more or less constantly. When anyone asks What happened he laughs. Fucking klutz, he says, I fell. It's nothing. But in his classes, while the students are working, heads bent over their papers, he loses time. Staring at the wall. Remembering how hot it was when his body hit the cement, the split-second sensation not of pain but of hardness, immense, unforgiving, against his face. How eager his flesh was to come apart. The bell rings, not breaking the spell.

. . .

The boy finds Bobby in the parking lot after class. Broad shoulders, dark hair, a bandage covering the remains of the terrible wound. The boy's heart going splash, splash, splash in his chest.

Hey, Jacob shouts, jogging across the lot. Hey!

Bobby turns. Knowing at once this boy is *the* boy. Sandy hair in his face and as tall as Bobby himself, five-eleven, but skinny, all arms and legs. Pants slung low, pale denim slashed at the knee, plaid shirt open over a dirty tank. White-blue eyes bearing down on him and Bobby touches his head, soft cotton and tape; still a headache, stiffness in his neck, a general shitty feeling which could last for a couple of weeks, the doctor said. Be patient. The boy is panting, lips parted, the toe of his sneaker touching Bobby's shoe.

Hey, Jacob says.

Hey, Bobby echoes.

I was at the pool, the boy says, sniffing into his arm, showing the pale crown of his head. How fragile it looks. Killable. All of them, no matter how young or strong, all these heads in the hallways, on the streets, on his own neck, ready to break.

Oh, Bobby says. Thanks. For . . . he gestures toward the bandage. Jacob nods.

Yeah, no, I'm sorry you fell. It was crazy.

Right, he says. Well. Long's doing his job, I guess. Getting you kids in shape.

Long's great. He—I mean he did most of the, you know—

Yeah, yeah, he says. Bobby is aware he's a bit wide-eyed, not acting quite right. The boy too close.

You feel okay? I mean they fixed the—?

Yeah, it's—just some stitches. Mild concussion. And the, the tooth. Bobby lifts his lip to show the temporary cap. Sheepish. He is vain about his teeth. Should be good as new in a few days or so, he adds. Weak smile. The car against his back. He wonders if he should give the boy money. Or a hug. He needs to figure out the appropriate gesture and then make it so he can go.

It was really weird, Jacob says, rubbing the toe of his sneaker against the gravel, glancing down and then back up.

Yeah. Scary.

The boy nods. Yeah. Staring.

Well, thanks again, you know, Bobby says. For getting me out of there.

He has to wait for Jacob to move before he can open the car door. The boy goes on standing there. See you, Bobby says, squeezing past him. The boy watches him start the car. Bobby backs out slowly. Waves.

One of the junior lifeguards finds the tooth and is holding it like a prize, showing it off in the locker room before swim practice. Jacob freaks.

You can't just take something like that, it's the guy's fucking tooth, man, you have to give it back, Jacob says.

Why? the kid says, smirking. He's got a new one, doesn't he?

Jacob's chest burns. In the end the kid doesn't give a shit about the tooth, he flicks it at Jacob's face and says Take it, psycho. But Jacob doesn't take the tooth to Bobby; it isn't Bobby's anymore. Jacob should have found it first. White on white at the bottom of the pool. People can't stay away from things like that, he figures, people can't keep their hands off something sick. Himself included. Himself included most definitely.

Bobby sees the boy in the halls. Roaming, alone, backpack hitched up onto his shoulder. Funny how he never noticed him before. Hundreds of kids he never notices. And now this one everywhere, never letting himself be looked at without looking back.

At night, Jacob gets stuck. Rolling the tooth between his fingers. Thinking about it. The water where it wasn't meant to be, the blood where it wasn't meant to be, everything mixed together. It's a mystery how he remembers things, some details lost and others crystal clear; sensations, sounds, not in order but distinct as slaps to the face. The splash, the screams, the kiss. Ms. Dean talked about *Macbeth* in English class that week. Something about spells. The water was a spell, Jacob thinks. He hasn't read the play but he knows the body is a witch. The water is a witch. A kiss is a spell, isn't it? *Jacob*, he hears someone call, *Jacob Jacob Jacob*. He must be dreaming, but the sound is far away, on land, and he can't understand what it means.

He gets Bobby's number from Long. He calls it. Bobby answers, says Who's this?

Jacob is panting, saliva whistling between his lips.

You know what it sounded like? he says. Your whole face hitting it, hitting the ground?

The boy's hushed voice gets into Bobby's gut and settles.

You know? the boy says again.

I don't remember, Bobby says. I don't remember any of it.

The boy swallows. I do. Let me tell you.

No, the man says, but the boy goes on talking and Bobby goes on listening.

Bobby can't get hard with his girlfriend. When she tries to kiss him he gets this horrible feeling, sick, dizzy, like he can't breathe. He puts his hand on her chest, pushes her away as gently as he can. Which isn't good enough for her. She calls him an asshole. He says It's the painkillers. Her face slips into a frown.

It's been two weeks, you're still taking those?

He shrugs. He just wants to sit in the bathroom on the toilet seat by himself until she goes to sleep. So he does. He looks at his face, touches the pink marks the stitches left in his head. God, he whispers, so close to the mirror his knuckles brush the glass.

. . .

It's weird being in Long's class. The girls give him these looks but he doesn't see them, he is lost inside the water, how it looks from above, sometimes like glass, sometimes like something else much softer. It shatters and gulps and winks and when Long says Let's do your drills Jacob just says I can't.

School ends. Their names in each other's phones, innocent, burning. They call, hang up, call again. At night when there is nothing to do but think of it: the moment right before the fall. What was it like, not knowing what would come next? The pool with its bright blue ropes, the black lines on the tile beneath the water. Jacob daydreaming on his ladder, Bobby's sandals flapping careless to the edge. That moment before the water turned to poison. Finally Jacob calls and stays on the line long enough to say Meet me.

They're parked in an empty Dairy Queen lot. It's dark, but the hot blush of July hasn't worn off and they are sweating, backs sticking to the seats. Jacob is talking, making the same circling motion with his hand, and Bobby has to remind himself that this isn't a dream, that he left his house unshaven, in his slippers, that if there is a moment he's been waiting for this is it.

    Look, I'm sorry about calling you all the time. I don't mean to, I just—

Bobby swallows. It's okay. Everything's really weird right now.

Yeah, Jacob sighs, his knee bouncing beneath the hem of his torn shorts. His hair looks dirty, a matted gold shag, and Bobby wonders what his own hair looks like, when he washed it last.

Does it hurt still? the boy asks.

Hm?

Your head.

Before Bobby can answer the boy's arm snakes forward, fingers pushing against the thick scar.

Does it? Jacob asks again. Hurt?

Bobby nods, wincing, his head pressed against the seat. Jacob's hand slides to the man's mouth. The pink plush lips, also scarred by the fall, the stubbled skin above them. The flavor of that mouth so fresh in Jacob's mind, iron and chlorine and fear. He can't stop remembering it. Tasting it.

Stop, Bobby says at last, twisting his head sideways. The boy's hands hanging in the air.

Why?

It's weird, this is weird. Trying to laugh but Jacob isn't laughing, he's rubbing his palm relentlessly against his trembling knee.

We have to find a pool, do you know where we can do it by a pool? Jacob says.

Do what?

Re-create it.

Bobby laughs, short, angry. You mean break my fucking head open?

No, not that, just after that. You get in the water and I get you out.

You couldn't do it by yourself, Bobby says.

The boy snorts. What do you mean, that's my job.

Do you know how much I weigh?

The boy's eyes darken. I don't give a shit.

You had help before, didn't you?

Yeah, but I didn't *need* it, Jacob insists. I could have done it. I could do it.

The boy looks at him, eyes wide. What's he like, Bobby wonders, when he isn't like this, bristling and hyped up and weird? What was he, before? Bobby will never know.

We could, Jacob says.

Bobby sighs. It's like you have a problem.

Jacob frowns. What problem?

Not just you. We. We have a problem. He peers out the side window, at the plywood nailed to the Dairy Queen doors. Warm air caresses the glass, slipping its fingers in through the crack.

It's midnight, Bobby says. Doesn't anyone care where you are?

Nobody, Jacob says firmly.

Well. That's also a problem.

Don't you want to?

There isn't any way we can do it, Bobby says. There's no point. He knows the boy is hard, he can see his prick pushing at the crotch of his jeans. There's just nothing they can do about it except tear each other's nerves to shreds. It's a dead end.

They sit there. How's your tooth? Jacob asks.

It's good, Bobby replies, quiet.

Hey, Jacob says. Do you believe in spells?

Bobby stares. A dead end.

He comes home. His girlfriend rolls over and touches his leg, slitting her eyes in the dark.

Where did you go? she murmurs.

Just for a drive. Go to sleep, he says, but can't take his own advice. He gets up and drinks a beer standing in the backyard with no shirt, toeing the silver seam of a snail track on the concrete. At some point you move on. Summer ends. You get through it without making any more phone calls, without leaving the house at midnight. You go to work and you see the boy in the hallway and you just nod and that's all you need to do. You get back in the pool.

Jacob calls and calls; Bobby doesn't answer. I saved you, Jacob says into the silence that follows the beep: I saved you. But the truth is, Bobby doesn't remember.

There's no security. Just a couple of lights glittering over the concrete. Jacob scales the chain link and drops to his feet, ankles humming with pain. He walks around the pool. Water glugs in the drains. The diving boards, pale blue in the day, bleached white in the night, hang like tongues over the water. The chlorine is like perfume, poison gas. He could get drunk on it. There's a shadow on the pavement where Bobby's blood had been; nobody would know it was there if they had not first tasted it, touched it. He kneels, puts his face in the pool. Drinks the water. Strokes it. Slips in, no splash, floating. Floating. It's not a bad way to go, he thinks. If you had to. He lets himself get heavier and heavier. Pushing out all the air. Touching the black line at the bottom. The witches stirring with their sticks. At some point you realize: you were always alone. And then rising, pushing up, a big breath, lifting himself out over the edge at the deep end. Curling up on the concrete, on Bobby's shadow, clothes pasted cold on his flesh, Jacob lies there and lets his love for the drowned man drain away.

FRANCIS

ALL THOSE bodies, heaped in the black sacks. Smell of death, lab-death, specific to this place, to these bodies, to me: piss and shit and fur and the bleach I tipped along the steel tables, the tile floor. Vast cloud of death-smell, invisible. I wear a mask but sometimes I take it off. When they arrive. One at a time. Touching their faces to mine. Tenderness. No danger, ever—they're good dogs. Chopped-down claws. Toothless. I am the man with the gentle hands, lifting them by the ribs from their crates. Setting them onto my lap. Shhh, I say. Hello. Shh.

No one likes needles. You don't need special empathy to understand that kind of fear, the rolling eyes, the shrinking.

They shiver. Twist. Mm, I say. All over. Stroking their ears. You have to know that by this time they are broken down. Before I ever get my hands on them. Still, I wouldn't do it if not for the money, if not for the fact that I can't stand the thought of someone else doing it. Saint Francis is what my bosses call me. Francis, they say. We have two more coming this week. And I say, brightly, into the phone, swiveling in my chair, the plastic gown I wear over my clothes crinkling beneath me: Bring them on down.

Every month or so a different set of instructions. Doses, frequency. I don't know what is in the bottles I dip the needles into, what poison they suck into their minuscule metal mouths. I don't know what it is supposed to do or not do. I know what the result is—those plastic bags. How heavy they become. Once a week someone picks them up, the same man, dark skin, dark eyes. Gloves. Strong enough to carry all the bags at the same time and lift them into a truck. I hear the door slam. The wheels on the road. The lamp outside the only light for miles.

At home it's just me and my deaf brother. Who can't work, who is home all day, watching television, masturbating, doing some kind of schoolwork on the computer. I come home and he looks at me. Waits for me to sign, to ask him what's up. Hungry for something. Expectant. I don't mind that look on the animals but I hate it on him. Have always. I can either make the sign or not, look in his eyes or not. If my back is to him he will tap my shoulder so that I'll turn around, so that I can start listening to him, watch his hands flutter and poke and pinch, inviting me to do the same. But before I turn, when I feel his finger on me, when I feel him waiting, I scream YOU STUPID FUCK. He knows I've said something, he can sense it, the vibration. Like a dog hearing something you can't hear. But he doesn't know what I've said and when I turn around I'm smiling.

I called the number from the flyer. The voice asked Do you like animals? And I said Sure. Such a cheerful voice. I felt very calm, writing down the directions. Long drive. No one there in the room. The plastic smock hung up, the mask. The jugs of chemicals and the directions taped to the green wall. It was clear-cut. Nights. Confidential. No vacation days. I waited for the delivery and there was a man for that, too, I learned, he had something covering his face every time I saw him. The crates, one at a time. The first time it was a dog so skinny I could see its heart beating beneath the skin of its belly. It just wanted me to hold it. I held it. The man said from behind his face mask You got it? and I nodded, mouth hidden behind my own mask, and he showed me the bottle I was supposed to put the needles in and I took that and the dog and carried them inside.

There's something about being in charge of something. Doing what you're told but also doing more than that. Having heart. Looking them in the eye.

. . .

Those needles, those bags, they translate one thing into another. I hate to see them go, their heads on my thigh, doing that thing they do when they take their last breath, shuddering, their world of feeling shrinking down to this tiny bubble of relief or giving in or whatever it is before that, too, disappears. I let them lie on me for a while. I go on petting them, saying things. The heat goes very quickly and that's one thing they taught me. How to look at people and think of heat. Even the worst son of a bitch is warm somewhere on his body and that's what lets you know he's alive. I open the bag, I clean up, I close the bag, I open the door and I go to my car and it's getting light outside. And as I start the car I feel that heat blooming inside me, the spot on my thigh where I let them lie, pulsing with new blood.

Sometimes I make a barking sound and my brother doesn't know what I'm doing. This gets me every time. He just doesn't know what it is to bark. Or to cry. When he cries he does it so loud that even with the bedroom door closed I can hear him.

An animal does its best. Anticipates your needs. Lies down. Keeps still. They can drink but they can't eat, these dogs. I don't know where the teeth go, who takes them out, exactly why. A muzzle would be easier. Or nothing at all— they wouldn't bite—except it's a liability, maybe. Maybe, if they could bite, their bites would be poison, the same poison I put into them, and then it would be me in a bag. I look up the sign for "muzzle" in my ASL dictionary. A hand clawed over the face. It scares me. I wait for my brother to make this sign, by accident, in passing, for no reason. He doesn't, of course, he's probably never signed it in his life. How many signs go unshaped by us? He doesn't even say as much as he could say. No one does. It must cost money to remove the teeth. It's someone's job, to do it, the way mine is using the needles, the way the other man's job is to move the bags. I wonder how many of us there are. How big this operation is. Each man in his room, on his route, taking the phone calls, making a mess, cleaning it up. Could be women are involved, too. But the voices on the phone are men's voices. The hands on the bags are a man's hands. The face in the mirror is my face. Every evening. Every workday shaving as if for a date.

The job doesn't stop with me, though the living stops, the animals stop. Something else happens, I'm sure. Some measurement. Some data put to use. There's a goal that isn't shared with me, an origin, a backstory. I'm just this one room in this one building on the outside of town where there is nothing for a very long time except road and dead grass and this table and these needles and these liquids and these bodies, one of which is mine, and I push the needles in and in and in.

It's no surprise that they die. Not even the first time. They come to me so close to it already. The liquids come in different colors, different dosages. Do they make it happen faster? Or slower? Last month I asked the voice on the phone Is it working? I'd been doing it for about eight weeks by then. Dozens of dogs. The voice was silent, but in an amused way, like I'd said something funny. You're doing great, the voice said finally. You're a natural, Francis. Just keep doing what you're doing. I hung up the phone and turned to the Doberman on the table, its chin against the steel, its brown eyes half-mast. You'd think the room would smell like dog but it doesn't. The chemicals are too strong. I rubbed its head. Put my nose in its fur. Breathed.

It's shivering. It trusts me so much at this point, it trusts that this, what we're doing, is its life. So it doesn't even try to move or beg me with its eyes to do something different. I put the needle down. It's not like there are cameras here, someone supervising, someone breathing down my neck. There is no gun to my head. I take the animal in my arms. I named him Bunny because of his long ears. Brown and ugly. Those lips wrinkled where the front teeth should be. I take him and I open the door and I put him on the ground. You can run, I say. It's warm outside. There's a little wind and in the dark, somewhere, the road. You'll find it, I say. He sits up at my feet, struggling, blinking, nose trying to smell something new. Trying to remember walking. Legs shaking. We take our time. I'm holding the door open, this heavy green door, metal, always cold. If he can hear something it's beyond me. There aren't any cars that come this way. Just us. Deciding. His breathing, loud. Eventually he takes a step forward. That's it, I say, casually, no pressure either way. He doesn't have to go. Doesn't have to do anything. It's just an idea I had. Bunny walks crooked, with his back up, like something is hurting his paws, like he can't really see where he is going. He moves out beyond the circle of light and after that I assume he's gone.

But later I find him by the side of the road. Didn't make it across. He was alone when it happened and that's how I know I messed up. I grip the steering wheel. Make a noise I have never heard before. But I'm not going to go mental. I learned my lesson. Freedom after a certain point is a mistake.

I have to drag Bunny back inside. So that no one will guess what I did. I prop the bag against the wall and lock the door again.

The needles rattle in my bag. One full dose and they're done. No convulsions. No knowledge. Just the eyes turning to glass. My brother is asleep on the couch, the blanket half slipped from his hip. Shirt rucked up so I can see the bare skin of his back, its sprinkle of acne. I think, Now I can be good to him. I know how. My hand on his side. For an animal, being toothless is a way of being dead. For a human, being deaf is a way of being an animal that is toothless. I didn't start it. I'm somewhere toward the end of the line. When the animals come to me they have already been somewhere worse before. Maybe it starts with being born. I could keep feeding him words with my hands, let him take the meat that is the stupid conversation we have every day. Drag along. I stroke his hip. He moans in his sleep. Shh, I say. Shh.

THE BROTHER

GIRLS OVERRUN the house like rabbits, or maggots, or weeds. Bianca, Veronica, Angelica, Janine. He calls them by the wrong names on purpose, reaching out blindly, *Biancaveronicaangelicajanine whichever one you are come here a minute.* He butts their flat stomachs. They crawl over him like puppies. We are always out of diet soda. Which is what I drink, or drank before all these girls pushed in with their elbows and their shrieking and their Victoria's Secret body wash smell. Even if I'm in another room, another house, another city, I can see him making up to them, those girls, their faces spangled with makeup, his fingers walking up their hip bones. They share the same cigarette, lying beside the pool, hands flicking ash, each mouth waiting its turn to embrace the lip-glossed butt. The smoke they blow rises, converges. My brother will jump from the nest of towels and cannonball into the water, spraying the girls, who shriek, their bodies curling like pill bugs. One by one he pulls them into the pool. Their legs grow together under the water.

So he likes women, my dad says to my stepmom. I don't see how that's a problem.

The one I want is Bianca, the small one, the one with an overbite and the prettiest hair. I don't want her because she is good-looking, though they are all good-looking. I want her because she seems to like him the most: she looks at him longest, laughs the loudest, wears the most provocative clothes. She is a link in a chain I want to see busted, and I don't want to wait for him to do the damage himself. Why should I? The hearts my brother will break are, for now, unbroken, and I want to break hers first.

The girls stand in line at the stove while my stepmother forks French toast onto their plates. They are wearing terry shorts in neon colors, tank tops, plastic bracelets. My dad looks at their thighs while he chews. My brother is at the end of the line, whispering to the girl in front of him. She giggles. They take their plates into the den and eat, draped over the couch. I can see through the doorway that he has two of them on his lap. They watch cartoons. The one I like is sitting on the floor between his knees; I can see her foot, curved around the side of the couch.

What are you looking at? my stepmother asks.

What are you looking at? I echo. My father slaps my elbow off the table.

Knock it off, he says. I press my fork into my French toast, squeezing the syrup through the holes in the bread.

Aren't you eating, Anita? my father asks my stepmother. She's drinking coffee. Her plate is empty. On the counter is an egg carton full of cracked shells.

There wasn't any bread left.

My dad snorts. Buy two loaves the next time. You know we have teenagers in the house.

I didn't know the girls would be staying over.

Really, Anita. Get with the program, my dad says, his eyes following mine into the den. My brother with his lap full of ass. My stepmother bangs her cup on the table.

We're not even related. His mother married my dad when we were ten. People look at us and don't think, *Brothers*. Friends, maybe. Or just boys standing next to each other by accident.

My brother resists a hierarchy; it's against their religion, he says, their spiritual beliefs. There is no best girl. They're all about equality. Free love. Like hippies, he says. You mean like Charles Manson, I reply. Whatever, he says, and I can tell he has no idea who I'm talking about.

I'm in the hallway, listening, when Bianca breaks ranks

on the equality shit; she wants him to go to a concert with her, just her, for her birthday.

Just for one night, she says, standing between his knees at the end of his bed.

My brother sighs. That wouldn't really be cool.

Why not?

Because it wouldn't, like, be fair.

It's just one night.

How about I get us all tickets? Front row! And dinner afterward, Olive Garden. Salad and breadsticks for all my bitches.

I can see, through the slit in the door, Bianca trying to take her hands out of his; he tugs her in for a kiss, but she turns her head.

Maybe I should have someone else take me.

He smiles his beautiful smile. What? You got four people to take you already, girl, dang!

She looks at him out of the corner of her eye and cracks.

You're such a pig, she says.

Come here, he says, and kisses her.

They are free. Free to tell him to kiss their ass, to stop fucking around. What is he, a prince? But they don't want to break up. They want to paint each other's nails, then paint his nails. He isn't callous or rude or a fuckup or an asshole; he *likes* them all. He gets them little presents, silver charms and sexy T-shirts with words like HOT BUNNY MAMA dripping over the chest. Girls fall for all kinds of tricks. Is it his James Dean hair? His skinny six-pack? The little gap between his front teeth? If you ask him about the girls, he holds his hands up like you have a gun on him: absolutely innocent.

After the girls leave I slip into my brother's room, sit on his bedspread, wait for him to finish taking a piss. When he sees me he shakes his head.

Why are you always, like, lurking, he says, and I get up so he can sit down.

I heard you arguing with one of the groupies, I say. She want to jump ship?

Naw, he says.

Sounds like she was pissed.

He shrugs. Not really.

I start flipping imaginary hair over my shoulder. You should like me best, I say, in a high-pitched voice, rolling my eyes up.

I do, baby, he croons back, and kicks my ankle. I embrace him, hard, an arm locked around his head.

Enough, he says into my stomach, shoving at my hips. I turn away, thumb through a skateboard magazine, push over a small stack of CDs with my foot. Tugging his algebra quiz from a textbook, I read the red ink: *68*, a D+. I smirk.

What'd you get? he asks, defensive, almost afraid. He doesn't like it when I smile.

Sixty-eight, I whisper. *Duh.*

We have the same teachers, take the same tests. I know the mistakes he would make. We both write with our left hand. He's looking at me, wondering what it means; it doesn't mean anything. He can go fuck himself. I drop the test on the desk and make a sound like a bomb dropping; when it hits it explodes. He lies back on his bed, one knee up, trying to act cool.

Better luck next time, I say, and depart. I close the door and stand outside it. He gets on the phone. I listen.

The boardwalk, he says, and I can hear, faint but distinct, the shriek of their combined *Hell yes!* I know his hand is slipped under the waistband of his shorts; I slip mine down, too. I smile when he smiles. Their sandals slap the steps. He opens the front door. From my spot in the hall I can see the shadows of their breasts on the wall. They use the bathroom, grab snacks, yelp when the dog licks their knees; then they are gone. My brother's car shoots down the street, hair streaming from its windows. They could die, I consider. He drives too fast. But then I would die, too, so I cancel that wish. *Let them live!* I sing to myself. My stepmom looks up from her talk show.

What, Kenneth?

Nothing, I say, and grin.

They come home, full of beer, half asleep. I'm pulling on Bianca's hair, both hands deep in the hot blond sheet of it. She just goes on wiping peanut butter off of a knife and onto a piece of bread. One girl is petting the cat with her toes and the other two are slung over the back of the couch, all legs and ass, and my brother is looking at me.

What's your deal? he says.

I just look at him as I touch the girl's hair, combing, combing.

Seriously, man, stop it.

You stop it, I say.

No, you, he says, blinking. I'm not doing anything.

I look at him like, Oh? The girl presses the sandwich together, takes a bite. My hands slip through the bottom of her hair into space. She turns to my brother, chews, pins her hip to the counter.

C'mere, he says, flipping me off with one hand while reeling her in with the other. The kiss he gives her smacks through the room, hits me in the mouth.

I take boxers from the pile at the foot of his bed; I take shirts, jeans, socks, and fold them into my own dresser, pulling them on at night, sitting in the dark in his favorite jacket. Their perfume rises from the fabric, having been smeared into it by their glossy heads, their restless arms. I don't want to take the jacket off. So I leave it on.

I'm fucking Bianca in the kitchen. It's dark and her back is pressed against the doorknob of the pantry. It's hurting her. In fact technically I am raping her, but she isn't trying to get me to stop, she's just hoping I'll hurry up. I watch the kitchen clock and time myself—they did it for eight minutes and thirty-six seconds the last time. So at 2:42 I come. We can hear the other girls in his room, laughing.

Close your eyes, I tell the girl, the one I want, the one I am fucking the way my brother fucks.

No, she says.

I put my hand over her face.

Jesus Christ, she says. Cut it out, Kenneth.

The other girls make excited yips. I know they are all in a heap on his bed and he is slowly peeling their clothes from their bronze skin. They go breathless, like lights turning down.

You keep drinking my Diet Cokes, I say to the girl.

Sorry, she says, rolling her eyes.

Aren't you going to do anything? Scream or anything?

She yawns. Not right now, she says.

You don't care?

I'm drunk, she says. I thought you were Mike.

You did?

She giggles.

I press the girl's waist beneath my palms. He's going to dump you someday, I say.

So? she says.

I stare. My brother and I are endangered; we are nearly extinct.

I withdraw. She wipes her thigh with a paper towel, tosses the towel onto the counter, then goes down the hall, opens his door, closes it. I listen for their voices: my brother says something and she laughs. I hold the paper towel in my hand and laugh, too, the way he does, but quietly, a whisper, my eyes wide in the dark.

JURY

THE COURTHOUSE smelled like mold. Martin sat with the heel of his hand over his mouth as the lawyers went through the prospective jurors one by one, dozens of them, himself in the last row. The air conditioner was broken. Shuffling feet, fans of paper, the suffocating stink of a hundred wet dress shirts. He was squeezed between a fat man and the wall; he felt nauseated. The hands on the clock wouldn't budge. He fell asleep for a few seconds. One of the lawyers asked him what he thought about the death penalty. He shrugged. He had nothing against it. The crime involved a young girl. Did he have children? Daughters? He thought of Quinn, on her last visit from school, sleeping in the backseat on the way home from the airport, fighting the flu. Her cheeks had been so pink, hot to the touch, just like they had been when she was little. She was often sick and she so rarely visited. He said, My children are grown. The prosecutor smiled. He was not dismissed that day, nor the next, nor the one after that. The trial would last four weeks. They would pay him twenty dollars a day for his time. He loosened his collar and sighed.

The day the trial began the jurors were introduced to the murderer. Not formally: he was just there. Middle-aged, tall and slim and strong-jawed, pale in his orange suit. His hands and legs were cuffed, a chain hanging between his wrists and waist. The jurors looked at him, at first in little snatches, then openly, at length. The murderer never glanced their way. Just stared at the stand, eyes hooded, his head tipped toward his lawyer. He was a completely unre-markable person, aside from the aura of evil Martin felt ra-diating from him, steady, unrelenting. If the murderer moved too quickly, if he coughed or reached for his coffee, the audience jerked in their seats. Martin watched the chain swing, then go still.

When he returned home his daughter was sitting on the couch, cross-legged, reading a textbook. What he'd told the lawyers was true—Quinn was twenty-one and rarely visited—but it was spring break, and he'd bought her a plane ticket. She didn't hear him come in and he didn't say hello right away. He wanted to take a shower first, get rid of the lingering sour smell of the courtroom, and then greet her, clean, murderless, but there was no way to avoid passing her on his way down the hall. He watched her for a moment, then two, her hair pooled on the pages of her book.

Hi, he said finally. She looked up. Her skin was very thin and smooth, dewy, and her eyes, sea-green, so serious beneath pale brows.

Aren't you hot? he asked.

What?

I mean you don't have the fan on.

She looked over her shoulder to the standing fan, then back at him. She shrugged. No, she said.

I'm sorry about being so late.

It's fine.

Did you get some food?

There was pasta, she said, and he saw an open container on the kitchen bar, three-quarters full.

Good, he said. I was just going to take a shower.

Okay . . . she said after a moment, in a low, slow voice, as if he'd said something stupid.

I'm happy to see you, he said.

She nodded, her eyes glittering in the dim light, before dipping her head back to her book.

The next morning they showed a picture of the victim's crotch, a splotch of mangled flesh made comprehensible only by the context of the gleaming thighs on either side, spread, perfectly white. The legs had been wiped clean, someone was saying, by the murderer. In fact all of the body had been washed, except for this part, this catastrophe, through which one could see premeditation, deliberation, intent. Distress rippled through the courtroom, hands stifling a collective groan. The murderer smiled a tiny solemn smile. I'm sorry, the prosecutor said, but you need to know what kind of person we're dealing with. Martin rubbed the back of his neck. The prosecutor clicked through more photos: close-ups, autopsy shots, a section of carpet soaked with blood. The girl's blond hair slipping off the side of the coroner's steel table. An elderly female juror vomited quietly into her lap. Another woman wept as she stared at the screen. The judge ordered a recess. The crying woman rose, knocking into Martin's knees. Sorry, she said, reaching for the wooden rail to steady herself, and as she did he glimpsed the wormlike marks on her arm, white and pink and purple, plating her skin from elbow to wrist.

There were sandwiches and warm sodas in the break room but only two jurors, the youngest men, were eating, silent, hunched beneath the fluorescent lights. The others watched the storm dump water into the street. The women were gone, presumably in the bathroom, getting themselves together. Man, someone said, running his hand over his head. That was completely crazy. Martin plucked at the cellophane on an oatmeal cookie and thought about the young woman's arms. She'd pushed her sleeves to the elbows, maybe to relieve some of the heat, but surely she knew that everyone could see those scars. Did the lawyers notice? Would they want someone like her serving on such a jury? You didn't get marks like that by accident, so organized, so regular, like the lines made on a doorjamb to measure a child's height. He got the wrapper off the cookie but didn't eat it. The clock over the door ticked and a clerk came in to say they would be excused early and for a moment no one moved.

It was still storming. There was no avoiding the rain that had risen an inch above the sidewalk; in one step his shoes were soaked. Martin rushed to his car with his jacket over his head. Through the windshield he saw the cutter standing on the steps, her stockinged legs dark with water, her hair plastered to her cheek. She was squinting toward the road, her lips pressed together. Rain flying right into her eyes.

He pulled up to the curb, shouting from the window. Can I give you a ride?

She turned, frowning, as if trying to place him. She looked back to the road, then to Martin, then to the road. Oh, she said, finally, yes, thank you.

She ducked into the car, using both hands to shut the door against the wind.

It's wild out there, she said, palming her wet bangs back from her forehead. She had narrow uneven teeth, very white, and a face like a slide, concave at the top, with a long slope of a nose tipping toward a prominent, squarish chin. Her eyes were almost black, like the sleek hair cut just below her ears, dripping water beneath her collar.

It really is something, he said, pulling onto the road. I'm Martin, by the way.

Jill Casey-Port, she said, offering a limp, moist hand. A hideous name. He glanced at her fingers: no wedding ring. She mopped her face with a tissue from her bag. The tissue disintegrated. He tried not to look at her arms.

Where can I take you? he asked.

She directed him to a neighborhood where identical stucco houses sat like squat blocks on cracked asphalt lots. He felt clammy in his damp suit, the air heavy and sour inside the small car. The cutter sat with her back not quite touching the seat, her hands clasped around her crossed knees. Only an hour ago she had been weeping; now she was almost smiling. He looked at her lap. Looked away.

It's just here, she said, indicating a bright blue house capping a dead end, tucked deep behind a crooked chain-link fence.

You don't have a car? he asked, checking the clock. It had taken him thirty minutes to drive her here.

Someone was supposed to pick me up, she said, shrugging, her face turned to the streaming window. But we got out so early.

She wasn't pretty. That strange sloping profile. Eyes too close together. A business student, she'd said. At the city college. She thumbed the strap of the brown vinyl purse in her lap and thanked him. No problem at all, he said. He watched her walk into the house. He wondered how often she did it, if she was going to do it now; he didn't know much about scars but some of the marks on her arm had looked fairly fresh, still pink. He wiped the corners of his mouth with his wrist. Rain drummed the roof. The fabric of the passenger seat was soaked. He touched it. Already cold.

He watched a movie with Quinn in the den. She had her legs tucked up beside her on the couch; he sat at the other end, an empty cushion between them. Skin, he thought, we are sitting on skin. Its seams dark with dirt. He never used the sofa when he was alone; he never used the den. On-screen someone squirted ketchup on someone else's chest. Quinn didn't laugh.

What do they call girls who cut themselves? he said.

Quinn was silent.

Cutters, right? he prodded. You call them cutters?

She blinked at the television. What are you talking about?

Cutters. Cutting. It's a thing girls do now, right?

Anyone can—

I know, I know, but it's mostly girls, isn't it? Who do it?

Quinn curled her back to show she was disgusted by this conversation. She did the same thing when they were eating steak and she cut into a piece of fat. If that happened she put her knife down, took a sip of water, and pushed her plate away, popping her lips. No matter how lean the cut of beef was she always seemed to find something, bent over her plate, spreading the meat with her knife and gazing into the dark gash.

I guess, why?

No reason, he said, shifting against the sticky cushions. I just wondered.

The cutter didn't say anything to him the next morning, just stood in the security line stirring her coffee with a red straw. She wore a gray long-sleeved blouse and yesterday's black skirt, wrinkled around the hips. There was a run in the knee of her stockings. He waited at the end of the line so he could walk into the courtroom with her. She smiled. No teeth. He smiled back. She took her seat. The murderer had laid his cuffed wrists on the table, pulling taut the chain attached to his waist. Martin couldn't believe the boredom that saturated him as soon as he sat down. The weapon the murderer used had never been found and it took an hour just to talk about that, what it might mean, what it proved or didn't prove. Martin pulled at his collar to get some air down his shirt. A forensics expert described the kind of weapon he thought would best make the sort of wound the victim had endured. They would not show the photos again, they promised; instead they used a drawing, black-and-white, full of numbers and arrows. The expert moved his finger eagerly over the map he'd made, describing how such and such a weapon would produce such and such a wound. You could fit the claw of this hammer very easily inside the entrance to a woman and pull upward with one stroke and this is what would happen. You'd have to hold the pelvis down with one hand, or maybe you could use your knees, crouching on top of the body as you did your work. But don't stop there. Keep ripping. You're strong enough. She was awake. For most of it. The murderer hadn't gagged her; he'd wanted to hear her dying. The walls of the basement were so thick. A lock on the door. Nobody home. The expert's finger zigzagged all over the paper. See here, he kept saying, and here, and here is where—

Martin squeezed his palms hard between his thighs. Shut up, he thought. Oh Christ just shut the hell up.

He brought home fried chicken for dinner. Quinn picked the skin off her drumstick and left it on the side of her plate, exposing a network of tiny black veins beneath the brown flour.

I'm sorry I can't give you a better time, he said as the rain slithered down the kitchen windows. I couldn't get out of this trial thing.

Quinn shrugged, licking her fingers. Her mother, his wife, had been dead for six years. An accident. Only recently had his daughter started this silent routine with him. He pushed a cup of Diet Coke toward her and she sipped it, a straw tucked into the side of her mouth.

School okay? he asked.

Fine, she said.

He nodded. Her gauzy gray sweater was rolled high around her neck but through it, at the chest, he could see the pale edges of a camisole. He used to know when she was on her period by the gamy way she smelled, the increase in intensity of her perfume. Now she smelled like nothing, not even shampoo. If he closed his eyes he wouldn't be able to tell where she was in the room. He closed his eyes. Dad, she said. What are you doing? He opened his eyes. There she was. He smiled.

He was drinking. Entertaining Quinn was impossible for him to do alone, now, with the trial and no wife and barely any money. It shouldn't be legal to put someone through this, he thought. The cost and the waste of time and all those filthy pictures and the family weeping in the front rows behind the exhausted figure of the killer, you could tell he wasn't taking any of it in or just didn't give a damn. His incomprehensible plea of not guilty. When there was all the evidence against him. We're stuck in the middle of this shit, another juror had said to Martin. It's sick. I get nightmares, I know I'm going to get nightmares. Just hang the bastard. But Martin knew that some of the others enjoyed it, striking serious poses and taking copious notes on their yellow legal pads, staring at the killer as if trying to show they understood something about him. As if anyone could understand something like that.

He finished the bottle of wine, opened another. It was 2:00 a.m. He would have to get up in five hours. His wife had been an early riser. He had rarely woken up with her in bed beside him. Quinn was the same way, up before the sun. She used to say she didn't like to sleep, she didn't have good dreams. When he woke up and saw them at the breakfast table, already dressed and drinking tea, toast crust on their plates, it made him feel like he was behind. He would spend the whole day catching up, walking into rooms where they'd been talking only to see them go quiet when he entered. There had been a car accident. In a storm. Quinn in the passenger seat with a broken arm, her mother's chest wed to the steering wheel. Quinn in the hospital shaking so hard her teeth rattled, weeping against his shoulder. Cabernet jumped down his chin and he moaned, setting the glass down, too hard. As he stood the table seemed to rush away from him. He coughed, moving down the hall to Quinn's room. Pushing her door open.

She was lying on her back, one hand curled next to her cheek, her body barely a ripple beneath the comforter.

Quinn? he said. He took three steps across the white carpet and bent down to look at her face. She was so still. If her chest was moving he couldn't tell.

He grimaced, holding his breath, as he peeled the comforter back from her body. She was wearing the camisole; her legs were bare. Clean. The mole three inches above her left knee the same as it was when she was a child. The round scar on her arm. Her thin underwear showed the outline of her hairless labia. He leaned and turned on the lamp beside her bed. Still nothing. He exhaled, pressing his palm deep into the socket of his eye, sickened, relieved. He pulled the comforter back up, smoothing it over her shoulders. A drop of red wine on the white blanket. He turned out the light.

. . .

My daughter came to visit, he told Jill the next morning, both of them sipping coffee.

Oh? she said.

Yeah. But I hardly—there just isn't enough time, because of this, you know?

Jill nodded, frowning in sympathy. How old's your daughter?

Twenty-one, he said, proud to talk about her, still: his daughter. A woman.

Ah, Jill said, smiling, opening a packet of sugar. Some spilled on the counter and she pushed it onto the floor with the side of her hand.

How do you get here? In the mornings? he asked.

She blinked. What?

Without a ride, I mean.

I have a ride, she said, her hand shaking on the Styrofoam cup.

You look tired.

She shook her head. It must be hard, doing this, when you have a daughter, she said.

Do what?

The trial, she said. She was so young.

Jill's hair was too deeply black to be natural, he thought. He wondered if there was a statistic somewhere, about who got murdered more often, blondes or brunettes. Time was moving in a weird way. Slower. Jill slid past him. There was a circle of coffee on the linoleum and he wondered if it was hers. He took some napkins and dropped them over the dark liquid, watching as the white fibers turned brown.

. . .

On Sunday Quinn sat at the table while he made breakfast. Eggs, bacon, toast. He'd said good morning; she hadn't said anything back. Just stared at him while he was at the stove, her feet pulled up on the lip of her chair, a black sweater stretched over her knees. He put a plate in front of her and she leaned away from it.

What? he asked. She shook her head, eyes slit, mouth set. Accusing.

Why are you looking at me like that?

She wiped her hands over her face and breathed. Last night, she said. God. *Dad.*

He blinked at his plate, his fork frozen over his eggs, a silt in the yolk oozing yellow.

Hm?

On the computer. Jesus, it was right *there.*

The wonder in her voice. The way she looked a bit beyond him, as if at a miracle taking place over his shoulder, the medieval kind, some saint tearing out its own eyes.

Is it some kind of weird fetish or what? she asked.

Fetish . . . ?

It's—really bizarre, Dad.

I'm sorry, he said, clearing his throat. He didn't exactly know what she was talking about. Whatever she had seen must have been from weeks ago, from before the trial. He couldn't remember the last time he'd looked at pornography. She had the wrong idea. But he couldn't correct it. It was his computer, anyway. Where was her own? The one he'd bought her? This was a girl with everything. And yet she never smiled.

She made a small movement with her head, as if to shake something off, the memory of what she'd seen or him altogether. Abruptly she stood, gathering her plate and juice glass, and took them to the sink. She was thinner, he noticed, than the last time she'd visited, the bone at the top of her neck jutting obscenely from the collar of her blouse.

Quinn, he said, eat something. She said she wasn't hungry. She went to her room and he thought she was doing homework but when he passed her open door he saw she was just sleeping, an hour after she'd woken, on her side with her back to him. She had always been a secretive person. He didn't know her. He touched the doorframe and a splinter of loose wood jabbed his finger. Jesus, he said, and her foot jerked against the blanket.

When he opened his computer the video began. A young girl, much younger than Quinn, telling the camera that she had just gone shopping. She had blue hair and purple lips, a black bra. She smiled and held up a package of razor blades. She opened the plastic with her teeth, withdrew one of the blades with a flourish. *Ta-da.* Now, she said, grinning, putting the blade to the camera until it filled the screen: Watch. She did each forearm, vertically, slow. She didn't flinch. Her skin just fell away from either side of the blade and blood surged into the trenches she'd made. When she was done she set the blade down, blood falling onto a sheet of plastic beneath her feet. There, she said, holding up her arms. See? Martin gagged. He had been drunk. He didn't remember looking for this. There were other videos in his history, from sites like *Little Cutterz* and *Bloodfuck* and *EmoXXX*. He felt numb. Quinn left the next day, before he even woke up. A note on the kitchen table: Thanks.

The murderer wouldn't testify. No family members of the victim testified. The defense was quiet, the murderer quiet. They were all going through the motions. At last the prosecution put the final pieces of their story in place; they had everything. Witnesses, experts, time of death, cause of death. Everything except a motive, the lack of which was the entire basis of the defense: Why? Why *this* man, *this* murder, *this* girl? Martin's legs kept falling asleep. *Because he is a piece of shit*, he thought. You just had to look at him, how he sat there, completely blank no matter what happened. It was so hot, with only a single fan to churn the stifling air. He tried to catch Jill's eye but she never looked his way. He spent the last hour imagining passing her a note on one of the legal pads. Something funny. So she would smile. But he couldn't think of anything.

He offered Jill a ride; they walked together, beneath an umbrella he held between them, their heads angled toward one another. She had dark circles under her eyes; the black skirt she wore every day was stained, the hem coming undone. There were water marks on the leather of her heels; ruined, he thought. Did she notice?

So how are you doing? he asked in the car, after a long silence.

I'm sorry?

With the . . . he circled his hand above the steering wheel and the car seemed to slip as he eased through an intersection gushing with water. With the, you know, just, the case.

Oh, she said, smiling vaguely at the road. I don't know. It's fine.

Really? Just fine?

She shrugged. I don't think anyone *enjoys* it. But we're near the end.

He rubbed his mouth, dropped his hand on the steering wheel. I worry it might be . . . harder, he said. For certain people.

Harder? she said, brow furrowed. What do you mean?

For you. Because of—what you do.

She froze. There were other things he said. The ride didn't end well. The next day would be the last day of the trial and he thought about this with relief as he opened the door to his house. He went from room to room to see if Quinn had left anything behind; she often did. Her note was still on the kitchen table. He took it to the kitchen trash; as he opened the lid he saw the greasy remains of Quinn's uneaten breakfast. He dropped the note inside, then removed the trash bag by its red ties and choked the bag closed.

. . .

It took them twenty minutes to deliver a guilty verdict. The murderer's mouth twitched. His lawyer just sat there. There was a wail in the audience. The girl, Miranda, had died thirteen months ago. Fucker's gonna fry, the Asian guy had said in the jury room, tapping his fingers on some papers spread over the table—evidence, notes, test results. The men were keyed up, loud. They had known from the start he was guilty. What a waste of time. Yet they had to be exposed to those terrible things, had been made to consume them, and now they would be turned loose, with no one to say how they should metabolize what they had seen and heard. There was something in the courtroom, something like slime, coming from that man, filling the place up. There was no getting away from it; soon it would cover them all.

It was completely dark by the time they were let go. He waited for Jill but she passed right by his car, walking with her bag over her head. In the worst rain of the season. Couldn't she call a taxi? he thought. That was how the girl had died—walking home alone, at night, after a shift at a bar. Can't you take care of yourself? he thought. Isn't there a damn *bus*? They were so helpless. They cut themselves, starved themselves, got themselves killed. He was doing his best. He was sorry about all of it. It made him sick. There's a doctor, he'd told Jill, the last time he'd given her a ride. She hadn't worn short sleeves since that day in court but he knew they were there. The cuts. She kept touching the inside of her elbow. It didn't seem like anyone was looking after her at all; she'd mentioned that someone, a man, had said he would pick her up, but he'd never seen any man, there was no man, she was alone. So he'd said, in the car, pointing to her arms, I know about this, I read about it, I know what you—and she laughed, once, in disbelief, and he reached for her wrist, to show her, that he understood, that she didn't need to hide from him, but she jerked away so violently her shoulder hit the window. No, he said, sh, wait, wait just a minute, but she spilled out of the car into the rain, the door hanging open onto the storm-shattered street as if onto a void, black, senseless, destroyed.

THE RAINBOW BABY

IT'S THE first thing anyone sees walking into the house; my lopsided head, bent at a weird angle, wide-eyed and grinning on a rainbow-colored quilt. In the picture I'm five days old, wearing a onesie that says SENT FROM HEAVEN BY MY BIG BROTHER MICHAEL.

You look like a total dumbass, Michael says. Jesus fucking *Christ*.

It's not my fault, I reply, and Michael makes me punch my own arm.

There aren't any pictures of Michael in the hallway, but there are a few in the Dead Baby Album. Sometimes when Mom thinks I'm asleep she sits in the kitchen drinking hot chocolate and paging though the ultrasound images until she gets to the picture of Michael after he was born, so small and blue against her chest, his eyes sealed, dead.

Wah wah wah, Michael says. Just listen to that cunt snotting away in there. That kind of shit drove Dad crazy. That's why he jumped ship.

That's not why, I protest. He—

Shut it, Michael says. What the hell do you know?

Mom doesn't know we're watching her. She squeezes her eyes shut, tears catching in the lines beside her mouth as she presses the album to her belly. Everything happens for a reason, she always says, but when I see her doing this I'm pretty sure she doesn't know what the reason is for anything.

Maybe I should go talk to her, I say.

No fucking way.

But she's sad.

So? Turn on the video game or I'm going to lose my shit.

I go to my room and start the game. Nothing happens, Michael just dies over and over again because he's not good enough at working the control and my hands slide all over the buttons. But he doesn't care, he just likes the sound the game makes when his avatar gets crushed by a rock or falls off a cliff.

Do you think she's still out there? I ask after a while. The house is silent and I imagine her falling asleep over the album, in the dark, all by herself.

What?

Is she still out there crying?

Probably, he says, and dies.

I can see Michael; not out in the world, but in my mind, and sometimes in the mirror. He has a normal-sized face but a tiny body, the size of a kitten. He can't make it do very much, and that's partly what makes him so mad all the time. God fucking damn it! he screams, trying to get me to reach for the box of Lucky Charms on the high shelf in the pantry. It's not snack time and I don't want to get the cereal down because Mom likes a routine and she gets this look on her face if we break it, a kind of crazy zombie look, her fingers dragging at the skin beneath her eyes as she yells I just cannot *do* this today! Michael thinks it's funny, but it scares me and I try not to do anything that will make it happen more than it already does.

Get the fucking cereal, he tells me.

Later, I say.

Just a handful, he insists, and I can feel his arm inside my arm, straining for the box. I watch my hand close around it, bring it down, open the top.

The marshmallows, he says, and I sift through the cereal until I have a handful of charms. He brings them to my mouth and chews.

We shouldn't, I say, mouth full.

Shut up, he says, you know you love it. I listen for Mom but I think she's in her room, meditating. I put the box back, folding the bag carefully so it doesn't crinkle. Michael sighs.

See? he says. That wasn't so hard, was it, douchebrain?

It isn't hard, in itself, just doing a bad thing one time, but he makes me do so many things. I get headaches, and at first Mom thinks I have a brain tumor and we go to a billion doctor's appointments. But when I end up not having a tumor Mom says its migraines and she thinks it's because I have allergies the doctors can't figure out. I tell the doctor it's because I get nervous. You're ten, the doctor tells me. What do you have to be nervous about?

Michael laughs. I shrug. You're fine, the doctor says, and then he opens the door to the waiting room, where Mom is, and says He's fine. But the headaches keep coming.

Every year we have a party for Michael. Mom wraps gifts and I open them. We sing and wear party hats and eat whatever foods she thinks are his favorites.

Carrot cake again, son of a *bitch*, he says. Michael hates carrot cake. I take a bite, but when Mom's head is turned he spits it into a napkin before I can swallow.

Yummy, honey? she asks.

Great, I say, squeezing the napkin in my fist. We open the gifts: a T-shirt with trucks on it, soft stacking blocks, a big stuffed bear—things for a kid much younger than Michael would be now, things neither of us would ever use.

Oh, that's nice, Mom says. Isn't that nice?

Yeah, I say, it's nice.

It's such a sweet bear. You can play with it. I'm sure Michael wouldn't mind. Aren't you crazy about that bear?

I guess.

Michael just *loves* sharing with you, Mom sighs. He wants you to be happy. Happy, happy, happy. She puts the bear on my lap. Michael laughs so hard it makes me wince. I push the eyes of the bear in with my thumbs, feeling how empty its head is beneath its fuzzy face.

How do you know? I ask.

How do I know what, honey?

That he'd want to share anything with me?

She looks at me for a moment, then back at the bear.

Of course he would. He loves you.

Michael hates me, I say, not really meaning to. Mom gasps.

Honey, what are you saying? Michael *adores* you, she whispers fiercely, leaning over the table as far as she can. He loves you *so much*. He's why you're *here*.

Tell that bitch I hate you AND her, Michael yells. Tell her she's an ugly old cunt whose womb makes me want to puke!

I put my hands on my ears and say Shut *up* and Mom claps her hand over her mouth and I say Not you, not you, but she isn't listening, she's just staring at me, and then she hits the table and shouts Go to your room!

Great, Michael says when I shut the door. Now that we've got that shit out of the way we can play *Death Hunters 2*.

I don't feel like it, I say.

It's my birthday. You have to do whatever I want.

You made her really sad, I say. I can feel him shrugging my shoulders.

She should be happy I hate you guys. That's what brothers do, they hate each other. And everyone hates their mom. It's normal.

I don't hate you or Mom.

Yeah, you do, he snorts, and turns on the game.

I come out of my room around dinnertime but Mom isn't in the kitchen. The cake and the blocks and the bear are gone—she probably put them in the nursery, which still has his crib and the baby clothes she bought for him and everything. I get a yogurt and eat it by the sink. Mom is pacing around in her room, on the phone with the psychic hotline. I wash my spoon and take another yogurt and leave it in front of Mom's door. Michael doesn't say anything. She thinks she's the only one who gets tired of eating and washing her face and getting out of bed in the morning and that's okay; I don't know what she'd do if she knew it was hard for me, too.

Babies are the worst. We always have to look; I don't know if Mom is checking to see if the babies are alive or what, but she literally can't not go up to a stroller and poke her head in it. One time we're in line to get Mom coffee at the café near our house and there's a woman holding a baby against her chest. It looks really small, smaller than normal, and it's wrapped in a blanket like mine in the picture, a big rainbow. Mom's face goes all red and she starts blinking really fast and I pull on her arm to distract her but it's too late.

Excuse me, Mom says, tapping the woman's shoulder. Excuse me?

The woman turns, her hand cradling the baby's head. Yes?

I had one—Mom starts to say, her voice very high, and I wait for it, for her to say Michael's name, to tell her about how Michael went to heaven and sent me instead, a rainbow baby, a miracle, blah blah blah, but the woman shifts the baby in her arms, dislodging its face from her chest, and we can see that there's something wrong with it—part of its nose missing, one eye closed and smooshed in—and Mom's mouth moves but no sound comes out. She steps backward, right into me. The woman folds the blanket around her baby, covering it up, and I don't look at her face because I don't want to see how upset she is; I feel like I never want to look at anything ever again. We leave without getting any coffee and as soon as we're home Mom goes to her room and shuts the door. I make a sandwich and turn on the TV and Michael doesn't tell me to surf for sex scenes or cop shows. He just lets me do what I want. Mom doesn't come out of her room and I imagine I'm alone, all alone, expecting it to feel weird and scary, but it ends up feeling kind of normal.

Finally I turn the TV off and get ready for bed. In the bathroom mirror I see Michael; he looks tired, his eyes redder than usual.

What the fuck are you looking at? he says.

Nothing, I say. I just can't stop thinking about that baby.

Michael groans. Yeah. What a freak.

At least you weren't like that, I say as I get into bed, pulling the covers over my head. At least nothing was really wrong with you. You looked good, you know? Like, normal.

I was dead, douchebag.

Yeah, but—you weren't messed up.

Michael's quiet for a while; when he speaks his voice is softer than usual. And how about now, huh? What do I look like now?

I see him, his weird body shrunken beneath that big head.

Good, I repeat. You look good.

The next morning I wake up with a headache. It's so bad I throw up twice, not even making it to the toilet. Mom comes in and starts pulling on her hands and moving her mouth like she's talking to herself and I tell her it's okay, she should just go to work, because she doesn't have any more sick days and her boss will be mad, and she says Are you sure? Are you sure you'll be okay? And I make myself smile and tell her Sure, I just need some juice and to sleep a little. When she's finally gone I go to the bathroom and lie on the rug near the toilet, my cheek on the tile, trying not to move at all.

You want to make it stop? Michael asks.

Yes, I whimper. Yes, please, help me.

I will. But you have to do what I say.

Is it bad?

No, it's not something *bad*, you baby.

You promise?

I swear. Now stand up.

I don't trust him, but I do what he says because at this moment nothing could be worse than what is already happening. The pain in my head fades a little as I reach for the sink and pull myself up.

Good, Michael says. That's good. You're doing great. Feeling better already, right?

I nod. He smiles. Okay. Now, you see Mom's bag? With all her makeup crap in it?

Yeah, I say.

Get the scissors out, he says.

Why?

Just get them.

I hesitate. A couple of years ago, in the middle of the night when I was still half asleep, he cut my bangs down to the scalp before I could stop him.

Get the goddamn scissors! Michael snaps.

I fumble through Mom's makeup until I find the scissors. I pull them out.

Now, Michael says, taking a big breath. I can see his eyes, blue, like mine are in the rainbow photo, exactly the same except bigger and more grown-up in how they look at me, almost like an old man.

We're brothers, right? he says.

Yeah, I reply. There's one big throb of pain behind my eye and my knees wobble and I almost drop the scissors.

See that? That's me doing that. And you know I can do it whenever I want.

I nod.

I don't *want* to do it. I actually really don't like hurting you. So. Help me out here.

I just look at him. He sighs and my hand jerks. The tip of the scissors nick my arm.

Ow!

Calm down. I barely touched you.

I try to open my hand but I can't; my fingers seem stuck to the scissors. Do it, douceface, he orders.

My hand shakes. I don't want to, I say.

Yes, you *do*. You want to help me, right? If you let me out, our problems are solved. But this is how it has to happen.

I'm scared of blood! I yelp, and now my chest feels like it's shaking, too; all of me is shaking and I can't let the scissors go no matter how hard I try.

Do you have any idea how much fucking blood that bitch lost when she crapped me out? *My* blood, *mine*, he hissed. This will be nothing compared to that. Nothing is going to happen to you. There just needs to be enough to get me out there.

I imagine myself on the white bath mat, bleeding, dead, and Michael in the corner, flexing his new limbs, slick as a seal, smiling a mucusy big baby smile. Mom would come in and he'd look at her, suddenly innocent, and step over my body so she couldn't see me anymore. He'd take her in his arms, let her cry on his shoulder. *Shhh, shh*, he'd croon. *It's me.*

Let me help you, he says.

I don't want your help!

The tip of the scissors darts toward my wrist. I hear the front door open and the pain in my head fractures, doubles, builds. A tiny line of blood appears when the scissors move sideways and then there is a lot more blood and a much deeper line and everything goes black. The scissors stop.

More! he screams. Hurry! You're fucking it up!

I can't, I tell him, and it's true, I really can't, and the scissors finally drop into the sink, cackling against the drain.

Honey? Mom calls. Are you in there?

Yeah, I call back, gulping air. Yeah Mom, just a minute, and I grab a towel and put it to my wrist. I can feel my heart beating in my arm like it's going to come out, but it can't, and if my heart can't come out then there's no way Michael can, either. We look in the mirror. Michael is sobbing, his shriveled limbs curled around his giant head, red and wrinkled and useless as he shouts You fucking butt blaster!

I'm sorry, I tell him. You're dead. I'm sorry.

Shut up! You shut up!

Please, I beg him, just leave us alone.

Honey, open the door, Mom says. Lunch is ready.

Don't, Michael hisses, don't you dare! You finish it!

I can't. I don't want to. I squeeze my eyes shut and I

imagine something covering his face, his body, a kind of black patch blotting him out. He was less than a pound when he was born, smaller than a person's hand. I imagine scooping him up and putting him somewhere outside, away from me, and closing the door. It should be easy to get rid of something so little and helpless, something that hardly even exists. But it isn't.

He goes on yelling. Shhh, I keep saying, she'll hear you, but Michael isn't listening and the door is opening behind me. I look in the mirror, to see what Michael thinks we should do, but it's only my own head there, pale and afraid.

Honey, Mom says, her voice rising in a panic, What *is* this—

Nothing, I say, I'm just—

But she's got her hands on me, yanking at the towel until it falls, revealing my arm, how red and open it is, and for a moment we both stare at the wound as it pulses, strong, alive.

What did you do? she whispers, Oh, my baby, what did you do, and Michael shouts *You stupid bitch, don't you get it? I wanted to live. I just wanted to live.*

THE LOVER

SHE WAS the only white girl at St. Therese, crouched in the yard on a strip of dead grass, whispering to a weed that grew near the fence. I stood across the street, in the mouth of Mick's liquor store, watching her. She wasn't pretty. Round face like a moon, thin lips, eyes too wide and too far apart. But that hair she had—gold and thick, all the way down to her waist—was something else. A fairy tale. She was eight and I looked about fourteen and when I went over to the fence to talk to her she didn't move. What's your name I asked. She didn't answer, so I answered for her: Margaret, your name is Margaret. Maggie, she corrected, quiet but not shy, deliberate. You know who I am? I said. She nodded, once. I tapped the fence with my foot. Raphael, she said. Yeah, I said. Ramie to my friends. She looked up, her eyes climbing the fence, and said Is it true you have a gun under your jacket all the time and I laughed. Yeah, I said. She didn't flinch.

It was five years before I talked to her again. I waited. I watched. That was all.

When the Dane came everyone thought he was one of the do-goody types from the suburbs who would stay a year at most. He wore these nice white shirts with the sleeves rolled up and ironed his jeans and smiled with half his mouth and never yelled or even opened his eyes all the way. He had a heavy accent and one of the kids asked where he was from and he said Denmark and the kid laughed in his face, not even knowing what Denmark was, but the Dane didn't care. He was like Maggie that way; only one or two things really got under his skin and most people never found out what they were.

With Maggie he knew better than to say anything. He squatted beside her at the fence, looking at her weed. It's a thistle, she said, and he took a cigarette from his shirt pocket and lit it. Which was against the rules. She looked up, smoothing the pleats in her pale neck, and he looked down, blowing the smoke to the side of her face. Yeah, he said. It is. You like plants?

She nodded.

He ashed his cigarette through the fence. Me too, he said. I lit my own cigarette, mirrored him breath for breath. His eyes met mine. I felt the nose of the gun, the one Mick'd given me, slide against the sweat above my ass. He stared. She smiled.

There are human plans and there are other plans. I was part of the other one, for Maggie, and even, in a way, for the Dane, and to some very small degree for Mick. But it was her I was here for. And she knew it. St. Therese hadn't been a real Catholic school for twenty years; the care center bought the building for the girls, none of whom had any real religion at all, except for Maggie. Retard Maggie. Slut Maggie. Bitch Maggie. The teachers thought she was stupid, because of how slowly she moved, how she never looked them in the face, even when they screamed. The Dane knew better than to feel sorry for her; I don't think he felt sorry for any of those kids. Which is why they liked him so much. But she was the favorite, though he was careful not to show the others, not even to show himself; he talked to her in the mornings, at the fence, he put his hand on her back when she passed through the door. That was enough. He kept an eye on her, the way I did, knowing she was different.

His first summer there they had a Fourth of July party, hot as hell and no shade at all, eating sandwiches and lemonade Mick gave them for free. None of the teachers wanted anything to do with Mick but when he gave you something you took it. The Dane was joking around with the kids, shooting baskets, imitating their dance moves, while Maggie drifted along the fence, watching. When the bell rang she stayed behind as the other girls went inside. The Dane was sitting on a bench, head tilted back to get the last of his lemonade, and Maggie went right over to him and touched his throat. Just put her hand on him and left it there. The Dane paused. Looking at her out of the sides of his eyes. She looked back. He put the cup down and took her hand in his and said You can't do that. Why? she asked. You just can't, he said. She tried to do it again and he squeezed her fingers, firm, and said No. Angry with her in his quiet way. Another girl would have cried but she didn't. Just stood there for a moment before yanking her hand free to slap his face. Hey! he yelled, jerking backward, and she ran to the bathrooms, her hair streaming behind her. Later he would go after her, hold her, let her say I love you, I love you. Her hot face pressed against his shirt. But for a long moment he just sat there, on the bench, looking between his knees as if he'd lost something in the dirt.

Two years later Maggie was fostered out. Packed up into the social worker's Honda, hair washed and braided, her hand clutching the strap of a brand-new backpack. The Dane waved from the curb but it was me she glanced at, me she gave the sign: I will return. Later the Dane saw me smoking on the curb and came through the gate and said You shouldn't do that. I flicked ash on the tip of his fancy shoe. He sat next to me. Asked for a light. But I wasn't one of his girls and it didn't suit me to sit there like we were friends, because we weren't, and I stood up and went inside the shop.

. . .

So much of my work was waiting. I looked older and older. Mick moved me up from security in the store to other things, anything, driving him around or picking things up or getting things he needed from people who didn't want to give it. Once on a job I got hit in the face and half a tooth fell out of my mouth and when Mick found out he hit me so hard the rest of the tooth fell out, too. So you'll remember to keep your hands up, he said. I remembered. I wasn't watching the school anymore or running into the Dane because he was gone, and St. Therese fell apart a girl at a time and the weed grew and grew.

She came back, nearly fourteen and thinner, her hair past her waist, a true blonde. By then St. Therese was done for, the building shut up and the kids parceled out to other shitholes in the city. It was Mick she came to for help, because she needed money and a place to stay where the people she'd run from wouldn't find her. I can work, she said, like Ramie, and Mick raised his brow and said You want a gun like Ramie's? And she shrugged, eye-level with Mick's chest—she was that short and always would be—but he didn't scare her and that impressed him. Look, there's a room, he said, don't worry about it. He folded a couple of twenties into her little plastic purse and gave her a chocolate bar. I showed her the room next to mine, sat on the cot while she folded her jeans into the particleboard dresser, a baggie of hairpins pooled against the mirror.

She turned. He's still here, isn't he? she asked. I told her I would take her to him. She closed her eyes. Happy. Come here, I said, and she sat down beside me. Looked at my mouth. Your poor tooth, she said. What happened? I shrugged. I fucked up, I said, and she smiled, knowing it was a lie. I wasn't capable of fucking up. Neither, in a way, was she.

The Dane was teaching at a school for rich kids and he had a nice little house with a nice yard and there was Maggie on his doorstep, in a blue skirt and canvas shoes and a big sweater, hands twisting the strap of her purse. Neither of them said a word for a moment. His eyes were red, his cheeks hollow. Well, the Dane said, and then went quiet again. Can I come in? she asked, and he moved aside to let her. He gave her tea and fancy crackers smeared with cheese and raw vegetables and she ate it all; Maggie ate whatever was put in front of her, even things like clams and artichokes, things every other girl she knew wouldn't touch or know what to do with. She sat in the kitchen, her feet barely touching the floor, and after a long while in that house of his he never married or had any kids in he said Can I see your hair, is it as long as I remember? And she undid it, pin by pin. His dog, a white whippet, stood near the stove and trembled. The Dane had changed, suffered something in her absence, and there was more room in him than before; she could see her opening and she took it without moving an inch from her seat. Just sat there and showed him that he could have her when it occurred to him to have her.

When I wasn't with Mick and she wasn't with the Dane we slept in the same bed. How can you stand it when Mick goes with other guys she said, touching the dark feathers on my wings. I said I didn't love Mick the way she loved the Dane. What other way is there? she wanted to know. She believed in things the way a child would, with absolute certainty; there was one true love and that was it. We sang along to the radio and I washed her hair and she lay with her head over the bed to let it dry, leaving a long stain on the blanket.

It was important to the Dane that no one see her come into his house, so she came only at night, through the back door, with a key he'd given her, worn always around her neck. After he fell asleep she would go out into the garden to pull weeds or pick snails off the vegetable beds, his garden more beautiful than any place she had ever known, even in the dark. When he woke up he knew where to look for her, going to the door bare-chested to watch her run her hands over the grass, smiling, before calling her in to make omelets, which she ate sitting on his lap, folding the egg in a piece of toast. Other nights he read out loud with her cheek on his thigh, histories or big novels, and they watched movies and ate dinners of pasta and fish. But then he would be done eating the pasta or reading the book and she would still be there. He was a loner, he was used to sleeping by himself, there were things he wanted to do, he said, and he couldn't do them with her staring at him all the time. Putting her mouth on his knuckle while he was trying to say something to her. Something important. Listen to me, he would tell her. Goddammit, Maggie, listen! And she would bow her head to show that yes, she would listen, she would be good, but she wanted to stay, and would he let her, and then she would be crying and he would be holding her and it always ended up one way, with his mouth on hers or her hand between his legs and neither of them saying another word and by then it was early morning and another night gutted, him unshaved and driving her home in the early morning, Maggie silent and burning beside him.

She got her period, breasts, hips, but her skin stayed the color of cold milk, no zits, no makeup. She never cut her hair. Mick called her the Virgin and she was, even after the Dane fucked her, though he skirted her hymen for months. We're in hell, the Dane whispered in her ear when it happened, inside her for the first time. This is hell. Though he was an atheist. She bled all down her thighs and he put his hands over her mouth to keep her quiet, though she wasn't making any sound at all, and he glued his face to her neck and wept for hours and fucked her for hours and she was lying there letting it happen, making it happen, her legs around his waist, somewhere beyond pleasure.

He broke it off again and again. She didn't argue when he threw her out. Enough, he'd say, ripping her clothes from his closet, his dresser drawers, her hairbrush cracking on the floor. This is crazy. You're crazy. I like women, I want a woman, don't you understand? His days were full of children, at the schools, needing him, adoring him, what did he want with one more, one who never left him alone, it made him sick, he couldn't take it any longer. She just stood there, watching him. What are you, deaf? he yelled. She called me and I came to get her. She'd fold herself up in her room and wait and eventually he'd call and it started again, harder, darker, those hours in the yard, asking him why he was letting the roses die, why the lettuces weren't coming up, and the Dane on the back steps, no longer smiling.

Still, she made promises to herself: they were going to get married. They were going to move to another city. They were going to have children and more dogs and a cat and a bird and two cars and vacation every summer on the coast. He had a koi pond and she lay on her stomach and talked to the fish. She had paper dolls he had given her when she was younger, and she still played with them, folding the dresses around the figures and trotting them up and down the pillowcase. We went to the movies and to the mall and played cards and I didn't let her smoke pot or get the tattoo she wanted, the Dane's name on her ankle; she was sixteen and she still listened to me. She still talked to plants. But she also worked the bar at Mick's strip club and she wore a black tie with her white shirt and cleaned the glasses and didn't say a word to anyone. The Dane didn't know about that. She said he would flip. There were things he didn't want to understand, didn't ask. Where she got money or how she really lived, dropping her off at the liquor store in the shittiest part of town. He pretended it had nothing to do with him. If she had wanted something nice to happen to her she would have chosen someone nice. But she hadn't. She'd chosen him.

He took her somewhere. Overnight at some campground. She borrowed pants from me, a heavy jacket, two shirts. She brought a bottle of Mick's liquor and they drank it all and he gave her a ring that was his mother's. Took it back the next morning, her screaming as he pulled it off her finger. Said he was drunk. That she was some sort of witch. Is it true what you said, she asked, by this time on her knees in the dirt, staining my best jeans. What did I say, he asked, stepping away from her as if from a snake. The back of his hand to his mouth. That you love me more than anything, she said. Get up, he told her, and it was like that time on the playground, when she'd touched him and he told her no; she got to her feet and hit him, and he took it, helpless, astonished by her, still.

. . .

By their third winter together he was spending his days at the kitchen table with only the stove light on. She gathered the empty bottles and trashed them, brought him more. Don't buy me beer, he said, I don't want you to do that, who would even sell that shit to you? She just set the bags in front of him, sat while he opened the next bottle. Mick's beer and her money. You need to be in school, he said. Drinking the whole time. He said You need to do something with your life or I'm calling the police. She smiled. Waited for the moment she could put her arms around him and he would let her, his nose tucked in her elbow, searching for the sweet smell beneath her white blouse. I knew that smell. It always reached me, no matter where she was. I told her not all men wept as often as the Dane. But you do, she said. You cry all the time. She thought it was because of Mick. But it was because of her. The way she sat at that table. The sound of those bottles in her arms.

The Dane left the school for rich kids where he was teaching. It was either that or they would fire him and he said to Maggie This is it. I have to go to these meetings and I have to clean this house up and if you love me you'll leave me alone. She said Let me help you and he said You can't. He was seeing another woman but was still coming to get Maggie at ten at night to take her somewhere to kiss her, fuck her, cry into her neck. Her hair was coming out in handfuls and she showed him the white patches on her scalp she hid with all those pins. Get some help, he begged. She slammed the car door, caught her jacket in it, ripped herself free. Walking off into the dark. Maggie, he called. Maggie wait.

Tell me what's going to happen, she said. I braided and unbraided her hair, in one row, two rows, three, my fingers working the satin strips. I saw her at one end of her life, a tiny white dot, pulsing; and at the other, enormous, searingly bright for one last moment, then blinking out to nothing. I don't know, I said. Pray.

She started dancing in Mick's club and no one was happy about it, especially not Mick, but she insisted, she was climbing up onstage in her busboy clothes and no matter how many times me or Mick dragged her off or slapped her face she just kept getting up there until Mick gave in. She kept her bra on and her panties on and looked the guys a little too hard in the eye. They threw money in her face; she wouldn't take the bills, wouldn't touch any part of them. That's what drove them wild. Their own willingness to put up with her shit, her thinking she was so superior. When the Dane found out—he followed her, he watched her dance and then vomited in the parking lot—he threatened to call the cops. I'm eighteen, she said, I can do what I want. She said Take me back. But he couldn't. Mick took half her money and she put the rest away in her drawer next to the paper dolls and the jewelry the Dane had given her, little silver bracelets and a barrette, Christmas gifts she never wore because they were too precious. Nine years and what he'd given her fit in that one drawer.

When she finished her shift I collected the pins she took from her hair in the palm of my hand. Her fingers crawling around her head. Loosening all that gold. I never did get used to it. Neither did the Dane. She hadn't seen him in three months. Raphael, she said, help me.

I came to his house. He said You're the one from the liquor store. I said yeah and could I come in. He let me. I said You know Maggie wants to talk to you. He got this look, angry, sick of her. I can't, he said, I told her already. Why I asked. He looked at me. Thought he saw me, but he saw only the mask I put on for him, little Ramie, Mick's bitch, skinny kid missing a tooth and spitting when I talked. He didn't see the wings, the solid gold inside me. Why, I asked again. She knows why. She knows exactly, he said, and shook his head. You kids, he said. You don't think anything's wrong with anything you do. You mean her working at the club? I said. Working for that fucking gangster, he replied. Wasting her life with a bunch of fucking criminals. I could smell the beer on his breath: Maggie'd told me he'd be drunk. Which I'd already known. I saw her whenever I wanted and I saw him, too. I'd seen them for years and years. Even before they were born. Maggie understood this but the Dane wasn't a believer and he didn't have any idea. You're a silly bastard, I said, and he curled his lip.

What did you want, Ramie? I knew at that moment Maggie was carving herself up in her bedroom. If I was quick I'd have time to see the light go out of her eyes.

You know, I said, God loves Maggie very much. But he doesn't give a shit about you. The Dane looked up in surprise. I showed him the gold. I showed him the gun. I kissed his mouth. Please, he said, and it was done.

AT THE SEA

OVER THERE is the child, a red shovel in her hand. Dig, dig! she yells. She's the only child on the beach still smiling. It's not hot enough anymore, the wind is sweeping the sand into everyone's eyes, couples argue about where to eat dinner. You roll onto your stomach and sip rum from a soda can. When your phone rings you don't answer. If only the child wasn't there, digging, oblivious, crusted with salt. Where is the mother? You are on vacation, you want to be alone. You put your hand over your eyes.

Later you buy the little girl a grilled cheese and french fries at a bar and grill. You should have made her wash her hands; now there's sand on the bread. She eats it anyway.

You don't have any dinner, you just drink. You drink and drink and she looks at you because you're not eating, you're not talking, you stare at the table or the bottles behind the bar. How old are you now? you ask, and this makes her smile. I'm three! she says, holding up some fingers. She's a good girl, you tell yourself, staring at her sunburned cheeks; she doesn't make a mess of the chocolate ice cream the waiter brings her in a plastic dish. You ask for the check.

You carry her on your shoulders because she seems to have lost the white sandals she had on earlier at the beach. She claps her hands in the lobby and a woman turns to look and you shrug because you don't know what the clapping is about. She does it all the time. Down the hall from your room is an ice machine that she wants to play with so you let her.

Look! she says, pressing the button. Chipped ice shoots out onto the floor.

Yeah, you say, that's neat.

You let her take a handful of ice back to the room. You have another rum and Coke while she pulls the cover back on the bed and spreads the ice around on the sheets.

Careful, you tell her.

She looks up and smiles. Mama? she says. You shake your head and tell her No, you'll see Mama later.

The rum, mixed with the cocktails you had at the restaurant, gives you a headache. You lie down next to the child on the bed. She's stirring the ice with her foot. You turn on the TV but you can't get the channel you want. Fuck, you say, then to the little girl: Sorry.

When you wake up your hand is curled in the damp spot on the sheets and cartoons are running around on the TV. The phone is ringing. In two hours you have to be at work; the little girl is gone. She's not in bed, she's not playing on the floor, she's nowhere. You get up, look into the bathroom, find her shoes. You answer the phone that is still ringing.

John. Did I wake you?

No, you lie. What?

Are you coming in today?

I told you, yeah, today.

Are you sure?

Well, Lisa, you say, and you know you shouldn't be on the phone, you should be out looking, trying to figure it out, the little girl, where did she go.

Actually, Lisa, I have to stay one more day.

John, what's wrong? Lisa whispers. Are you sick? You sound sick. What's going on?

No, I—just, I'll call Friday, okay? I'll call tomorrow.

It's very hard to say anything else. You're still drunk. You hang up. You sit for a moment. There's a rustling under the bed and you shout Hey, hey! You bend down to look and there she is, smiling at you, giggling. You're angry, then you're happy, then you're sad. She crawls onto your lap and pats your cheek and says Oh Daddy, don't cry.

EVIDENCE

HE STEPS around the body and its shadow of blood. The head, where's the head? He leans closer: some kind of mashed in. Pulverized. But it's all here. Kneeling, he sniffs, pokes, prods, guesses, wonders, looks. A bit of brain like putty dried on the oven door. One of the cops whistles. The detective stands. Peeling off gloves, giving orders. Pages of notepads flickering. Making the usual jokes. He turns his back on the other guys, rubs his eyes. Somehow he is expected not to go crazy. Blood even on the flowered wallpaper. He squints. The flowers and the blood compete for white space. He is sure a woman was here. Red prints on the linoleum left by a pair of pumps.

Detective, someone says. He is leaning so close to the wall he can smell the grease and blood breathing from it. Bouquet. He shuts his eyes, thinks of something far away. Fields. Humanless. Green.

Detective?

What? he says.

You better take a look at this.

He opens his eyes. The fields vanish.

After his shift he sits in his car. He's looking at a house and thinking what kind of person would leave their living room window open so late at night in this crazy neighborhood and then he realizes this is not a house he's casing, it's his actual house.

A beautiful woman being dead never surprises him. Murder looks less cheap on a pretty woman: it can look like a million bucks. She could be flung across a bed, hair a flame on the sheets. Curled somewhere, dainty, maybe in the back of a car, blood drawn by the pinch of a knife, or a necklace of bruises high and dark on a slender throat. It never looks like an accident. The eyes are never closed. If she's beautiful, she sees it coming.

The detective tells his wife these things after dinner. He says it while tapping ash on the tablecloth and gesturing to conjure these women, to show her, see, this one and this one and this one, all beautiful, all dead, but not you, thank God, you were never beautiful.

The wife hugs her elbows across her chest. I want a divorce, she says.

Maybe I'm getting confused, he says. About the women, I mean.

Confused? His wife's voice rises as he tilts his plate to look beneath it, causing the unfinished steak to slide in its skin of blood.

Okay, okay. I'm sorry. He sets the plate down. The steak rests.

You don't even know what for, she says, and then she's gone.

He is called in to a scene where a boy is hanging in his father's closet next to a rack of pants and a lot of laundry piled on the floor. The detective eases sideways into the closet to get a look at the face that is drifting away from him: ears cheek chin, silk of tie and tongue, and then the wide green eyes. The detective jerks back and says Aw, shit.

What? his partner asks. The detective is pinching the bridge of his nose, hand on one hip, shaking his head.

Oh fuck, you know him?

Sort of, the detective replies. Used to mow my lawn. Justin somebody.

No shit, his partner murmurs. They rummage through dressers, beneath beds, in coat pockets, but everything is missing. No note, no drugs, no foul play. The detective looks so hard his eyes hurt. A photographer comes in and the flashes go off like slaps.

You know it wasn't my fault, the mother says. The detective scribbles on his notepad and makes a noise that means We'll see.

The man with the mashed-in head didn't have a girlfriend. Ex-wife accounted for two hundred miles away. No sisters, no nieces, no internet or credit card or cell phone history of contact with suspicious persons—hookers, drug runners, best friend's woman. The house is clean of condoms. No history of his knowing anyone who would wear such fancy shoes. Size seven. Too small for a cross-dresser and the only other shoes that made prints are on the dead guy's feet. Weary blob of blood on the welcome mat and after that, nothing. Leading to nowhere. Would have been blood in the shoes, down the legs, all over her. No sign she ran the shower or even used the sink. No witnesses reporting a woman going inside the house then coming out drenched red. The detective got on his knees near the stove, measuring the prints next to his hand.

Pointy toe. Smooth sole. High heel.

The detective keeps a photo of the dead man's head; there it is, intact, stuck to a bulletin board. *You're going to die*, the detective thinks every time he looks at the ugly happy face. By this time his own house is officially empty of family, as clean as an old crime scene. He watches all the shows with cops in them so he can remember how to act. He frowns, he drinks coffee, he tells dirty jokes. He strokes the glossy photo and thinks of all the women he has known, all the meat inside a man. How often it is the other way around: the woman in pieces, and every man a murderer.

She's about the age he guessed—thirty, thirty-five. Young people, unless they are on drugs, don't have enough rage to do what she did. And the shoes, four inches, the dress, white: he just gets a feeling sometimes. In the guts. Halter strap cutting into her neck as she turns to look at who walked in and then turns again when she sees it's just him. His badge burns in his jacket pocket. He hitches a hip onto the stool beside her and she concentrates on squeezing a lime into her beer. He looks and looks at her. Big beautiful face, cheekbones, no makeup and she doesn't need it. She looks back: cutting eyes. Cruel. Capable.

Don't, she says.

Don't what?

She leaves the dry lime in a fetal curl on her cocktail napkin.

I'm surprised you haven't left town, he says.

She rolls her eyes.

The bartender asks him what he wants and he says Martini and when the woman snorts he says No, I mean beer, sorry, did I say martini?

The bartender uncaps the beer on the edge of the bar and the steam that rises from the bottle is like smoke from a lazy fire.

I just want to know one thing, he says, but she gives him nothing, no sign she can even hear him. He reminds himself he's been here before: Take it slow. Smile, lean in, get cozy. Approximate admiration. A perp leaves a body like that, you better pretend you're impressed.

Helluva job, he says with a chummy smile. What you did. Really first-rate. Must have been a real asshole for you to do it like that.

Do what, she says.

I know, I know, he says, you have your reasons. But there are simpler ways, right? Why the thing with the head?

Her neck stiffens. Is this some kind of joke?

He shows his palms. Easy, I'm just asking you an honest question.

Jesus, you're drunk already.

I'm a cop, he whispers.

She smirks. Next you're gonna tell me I'm under arrest, right?

He imagines cuffing her strong wrists. Steel jewelry jangling against her white skin, chafing the blue veins. The flowered paper, the blood already dry. Flowers used to make him think of perfume. Not anymore. He misses a beat. Comes back.

You didn't leave a single good print, he says, wagging his finger. But you forgot about the shoes.

What the fuck, she sighs, lips pillowed against the mouth of her beer.

We learn in school, he continues, what marks all the different types of shoes make. I recognized yours right away. Not definitive proof, but definitely incriminating.

She drains her beer, asks for another. He hasn't tasted his own drink, or if he has, he doesn't remember. She peels the label from her bottle, the glue and the paper scratched from the glass with her thumb. He imagines her stroking a weapon, though he can't remember what it was: a bat? A knife? A gun? Nothing was ever found, the case gone cold, freezing. He watches her, hoping she can at least melt the edges off.

I never saw anything quite like it, not from a woman. He rubs his nose, sniffs. I admit, it got to me. Is still getting to me.

So I killed him, huh? she says, and suddenly he's changing direction, hotshot just like in the movies, keep it cool, you got her where you want her.

I don't know. You tell me, he says, leaning back on the stool, wiping the bar with his hands, catching a glimpse of himself in the mirror behind the bartender: all shoulders in a sagging suit. A slice of unshaven chin.

Let me guess, she says, her palm falling hard to the bar. Out of work? Health troubles? Bad luck? Nothing nice happens to you or what?

I've seen a lot of bad things, he explains.

Well I've seen things too, she says, offended, like he's trying to keep all of something valuable to himself.

That's no excuse in the eyes of the law, lady, he says.

She gets off her stool, gathers her purse from the floor. Her heel makes a cracking sound on the tile. He flinches.

I don't really have time for this, she says.

When she comes out of the ladies' room he is there; she has to step back to keep from running into him.

I don't want to fuck you, she says. Get it?

I know, he says humbly.

Then what do you want?

He kneels to grip her skirt. The whiteness of the dress baffles him, saddens him: the man had been splashed all over that kitchen. There should be a trace, some mark on her, a scar, and yet: this dress. Its whiteness. The woman's strong legs.

Do you think I feel sorry for you? she says, not unkind, looking down.

Why can't you? he says.

Why should I?

The skirt wrinkles, folds in his hand.

How did you get it out? he says. All that blood.

She shrieks, disgusted, as their hands fumble in the field of her skirt, hers trying to pry him off, his trying to hold on. Thinking of the man's head, his own head, what he'll never get back.

Please, he begs, please, I've seen enough, just do it to me too.

VIRAL

I'M IN the car waiting for my boyfriend to kill her. It's 2:00 a.m. and Veronica's neighborhood is completely quiet. No one will see him, with his stupid hoodie and the black hair I dyed last weekend falling into his face, scrambling through the hedges to her front door. No one sees me, slouched in the backseat, the sleeve of my jacket tucked deep inside my mouth.

Six weeks ago Blake asked Veronica for her phone number. Blake is a terrible student, a total slut, and definitely not her type. No boy is really Veronica's type. But he didn't get it; he was tall and zitless and looked like the vampire in the *Twilight* movies and had always got any girl he wanted. So when she just stood there, polite but aloof, he didn't know how to play it. Hey, he said, half smiling. We should hang out sometime.

Veronica shook her head. No, sorry, I don't think so, she said, touching his shoulder before moving past him to the curb, where her dad was waiting in their silver Mercedes. Suddenly he looked ridiculous, even to me, standing there with his mouth open in his tight pre-ripped jeans and fake leather jacket. All around there was a rustle of laughter, like candy bar wrappers being crinkled beneath a desk. Fucking bitch, he muttered, lighting a cigarette and throwing the match into the grass before walking away.

The first time I saw her do it we were eleven. I was at her house for a sleepover, taking a bath, washing my hair with her fancy shampoo in the deep tub. She was the only girl I knew who had her own bathroom. I dipped my hair beneath the water to rinse, pretending I was a mermaid with the longest hair in the kingdom. When I sat up I heard something through the door, a sound I recognized; at a certain age you know every kind of creak a mattress can make when a body is on it. I got out of the water very carefully, dripping on the thick white rug, listening. The sound was rhythmic, soft; I pulled a towel from the bar and wrapped it around my chest, creeping over the rug to the door. I turned the knob slow, so it wouldn't make any noise. Veronica was on the bed, facedown, the head of a Cabbage Patch doll between her legs. Her nightgown was pulled up to her waist and I could see everything: her ass clenching, hips pumping, knees driving into the blanket. Heat swallowed my crotch. It went on for a minute, two minutes, before she went still, gasping into her pillow. I stepped back. As I was closing the door my hand slipped on the knob and the bolt snapped into place like a shot.

Zee? she called in a bright, breathless voice. Are you ever going to get out of that bath?

Yeah, I called back, equally breathless, pulling on a T-shirt. I'm just getting dressed.

When I came back out she smiled nervously, flushed. We ate ice-cream sandwiches, watched *Anne of Green Gables*, then went to bed; I slept on the floor. After that we weren't really friends anymore and I never spent the night at her house again.

He came over the night after she turned him down. I was wearing a cropped shirt and the same purple lipstick his last girlfriend had worn, but he didn't say anything about how I looked. He never did. He just sat on my bed playing with his phone for an hour while I watched him.

We could get her back, I said finally.

Yeah? he said, looking at me for the first time that night. How?

I gave him a bottle of vodka my brother kept in the freezer and told him my plan. He kept the vodka between his legs and when I wanted a sip I would put my mouth on the bottle like I was going to give him a blow job and he said Go on, you alkie, drink it. I did. His thighs were cold. I'd never touched his bare legs. He leaned back on his elbows and watched me move the bottle from his lap to my lips to the floor. His eyes were slits, but I could see the blue beneath his lashes, sparkling at me. You really want to? he said. I unzipped his shorts, about to cry. Okay, he said, barely moving his mouth, nodding like he was going to fall asleep, but he didn't, not until he finished and I was wiping my lips with my wrist.

I sat behind her in homeroom. *Veronica*, I hissed. *Veronica!* I waited for her to turn around, to look at me, to smile, but she didn't. Maybe she hadn't heard me. I wrote on a piece of paper *You're a bitch* and folded the paper until it was a tiny square no bigger than the tip of my finger and when the bell rang and she walked by I flicked it off my desk in her direction. It hit her calf and fell to the floor. I caught her eye and she waved at me, like she would to anyone else, and kept walking.

The plan was we would film her fucking the doll. Blake asked how I knew she still did it that way, and I didn't know, not for sure, but I was willing to bet that when she really needed to get off this was how she did it. He didn't ask why I hadn't told him that I'd been friends with her; he probably thought all girls were friends, in a way, at some point. What I think about is how much she must have wanted it that night, enough to do it while I was there, just behind the door. When I need to come fast this is what I imagine. Not a boy. Not Blake. Just her hips, her face, the little sound she made when she came, the terror in her smile when she knew she'd been caught.

He doesn't know what he's doing, what it means. How can he? He only thinks five minutes ahead. That's why he needs me: to think through how to use the video I'd shot. Why to shoot it in the first place. I knew when her parents were going to be out of town and that she would be staying home alone—they'd been leaving her alone overnight since she was thirteen. She's a good girl. They trust her. And Blake trusts me.

In the videos her room looks the same. I can still remember how it smelled—like furniture polish and fabric softener and lavender candles. She even has the same bedspread, white with purple flowers. In the first video she's sitting on it, her back against the pillows, a book open against her thighs. A glass of water beside the bed. She reads and then just goes to sleep, lights out, nothing. We turned off the camera, climbed down the tree we'd used to get to her balcony. You better not be fucking with me about all that shit, Blake said in the car, slamming his door. This better fucking happen. I told him that I wasn't, that it would. He stared at me and I stared back. We could have had an argument but we didn't. We stayed up half the night, not kissing or messing around, just lying side by side on his bed watching beheading videos.

Does she know you know? he asked. About what she

does? I was almost asleep. I didn't answer. Zee, he said. I pretended I was dreaming and muttered something he couldn't understand. He sighed and shut his laptop, turned out the light.

In the final video she's reading again, but this time she's on her stomach, her head propped on her hand. Thirty seconds into the film she starts rubbing her hips against the quilt, just barely at first, her ass quivering beneath her nightgown. She does this for a while, reading and doing the thing with the blanket, and then she puts the book down and reaches under the side of the bed, her legs parted so there's just a glimpse of what's between them. When she rises she has the doll in her hand. Something in me clenches. It hurts. She stuffs the doll beneath her hips and lowers her head and I'm holding the phone very hard in my hand, right in front of my face, but I'm not looking at the screen, I'm looking directly at her. She doesn't even turn out the light. She thinks she's free, that no one will bother her. No one has ever really bothered this girl. And that's when I'm really sorry for her, because it's so stupid and so sweet and so sad. Blake laughs in disbelief and I shut him up, wishing he hadn't come. It goes on for eight minutes and thirty-two seconds. You can barely see the doll beneath her but because you already know it's there the doll seems more visible than it really is. Its blond braid struggling from beneath Veronica's pumping hips. When she's done she just lies there, her head turned to the window. I zoom in as much as I can and the screen fills with a grainy close-up of her lips crushed against the pillow. Then she slowly sits up, a loop of hair sticking out from her head; she puts the doll back under the bed and reaches for the lamp.

We upload the video straight from the phone, no computer. We send it to the law firms her parents work for. We send it to the school principal. Facebook, Reddit, Twitter, YouTube, RedTube, 4Chan. VERONICA MINKLEN'S FIRST FUCK. We wipe the phone with bleach when we're done, then we throw the phone into a canal. There's nothing of us in that video except the sound of our breathing and Blake saying Holy shit and some slushed laughter that doesn't really sound like us at all. It's laughter that comes from everywhere, from nowhere. You've heard it. At some point it's had your name all over it.

After we shot the last video we had sex. I didn't tell him I was a virgin and when he got inside me I bit his shoulder to keep from screaming. When the burning feeling stopped there was nothing to replace it, just him going on and on above me, his eyes squeezed shut. I turned my head to look at the window, to see if the blinds were closed, and for a moment I saw Veronica right there, in the bed with us, smiling. I made a noise and Blake said Did you come?

She can't see the car from her room. She wouldn't recognize it if she could, and she wouldn't recognize me, with my hand covering most of my face, in the dark beneath the trees. It feels like it's taking him a very long time to do this simple thing and I just want it all to be over with. I don't hate her. I don't particularly want her to die. But he despises her. She is pretty and very smart and she didn't want to go out with him and sometimes it's as simple as that. In a few minutes, when the doorbell rings, she'll see the note he is pushing beneath her door. She'll go to her computer and type in the URL we've given her. There's nothing she can do. Everyone, including her, will know that she is trash because we will have made her trash. There is no one in the house to stop her from doing what she's going to do next. Blake thinks it's just a joke, that Veronica will freak out for about a week and then get over it. But I know the pride inside her, what a virgin she is to any real pain. I know she'll do it. We were friends, after all.

THE SHUT-IN

THERE WAS no car in the driveway. No television noise, no lights behind the curtains. I never saw anyone go in or out. But the house wasn't empty. You can always tell. The pressure of living, no matter how small, pushes out from a place. Did it know I was there, as soon as I arrived? Did it watch for me as I watched for it? I was quiet, too; I hardly moved, at home. I didn't have enough furniture to fill the two tiny bedrooms. I ate on the couch, a paper plate on my knees. I was twenty-two. It was my first time living alone.

I stood in the Walmart for a long time trying to decide about a backpack, what color it should be. I fingered the blues, the greens, the purples. What did a color say about you?

I imagined myself with each one but walked out with the cheapest black bag they had.

People will happily not talk to you in college. And not on purpose, not because they had already talked to you and not liked what you said, not because not talking to you was part of a plan, as it always was in high school, but because you were an adult and you were paying for everything and you had responsibilities beyond making friends and enemies. At the college there were plenty of people with black backpacks just like mine. It didn't mean anything. I sat like a rock at the back of my classes, surrounded on all sides by a line no one ever crossed. It was hard for me to understand anything the teachers said because I was so aware of this phenomenon. Nobody knew me. Nobody was going to know me. Would it crush me? I wondered. Did I want to be crushed?

I took a piece of paper from my bag and wrote the shut-in a note: *Hi, I am your neighbor I live across the street. I noticed you don't go out very much. Well since I am new here neither do I. If you need something you can write me a note. I will put this under your door and hope you will not consider it trespassing. Sincerely Lee Cross.*

I folded the paper in half, then in half again. I held it in my lap and smiled.

There was no real grass in the shut-in's yard, just brown weeds pulped up in the dirt. In the gaps of a dead hedge junk clung to the walls of the house: plastic patio furniture, an old sink, empty black planters. I opened the screen door and stared at the plywood behind it, my fingers stroking the loose bronze knob. There was nothing coming from inside the house, no light or sound at all, but I was quiet, listening, and after a while I felt it: that tingling in your gut that tells you that you are not alone. I knelt, pushing the paper beneath the door; it whispered across the floor. I panicked for a moment, huddled on the step, the screen against my side, worried the note might say something I didn't remember writing. But it was too late. I pressed my hands against my eyes.

The next day I got some food at the gas station near the bus stop. There were plastic sleeves of donuts at the front counter, two for a dollar, and I picked up a couple, wondering what the shut-in ate. It could have stocked up a long time ago on something, canned food or frozen things. Or maybe it got stuff delivered and I hadn't been around long enough to see anything arrive. Maybe the shut-in ate nothing at all anymore, I thought, though I knew that wasn't possible, unless it wanted to die, was dying right now. I ate only packaged foods. Canned ravioli was best, but it was expensive. The check I lived off of was broken down into other checks, to pay bills, and the little cash I withdrew seemed to turn immediately into loose change. My hands always smelled like quarters. If you never left the house you probably never touched money at all, I thought, it would lose some of its power, you would almost forget it existed. It was probably like that with a lot of things. I picked out two more packages of the donuts and paid.

What is your favorite color? I always choose black but it isn't my favorite. I don't know what my favorite is.

I took the donuts to the shut-in. I knocked on the screen door, soft at first, so that the metal barely trembled. Hello, I said, almost to myself. No sound came from inside. Hey, I said. It's me. Your neighbor. I stopped knocking, set the donuts down on the step. Hey, I said again, louder. I'm a nice person, I thought. Nice enough. I dropped my fist and listened. A breeze made my hair feel like bugs crawling over my face; I scratched my forehead. There was a sound, suddenly—some part of the house, creaking. Footsteps. No thumping, no shuffle—its steps were slow but clear—no cane, then, no wheelchair. I could hear it bend down for the letter, its fingers on the paper. Would I be ready, if it opened the door? I tapped on the plywood. It tapped back, slow, echoing me. You can hear? I said. It tapped. You can see? It tapped again. You got my note? Tap-tap. Its breath was uneven, harsh, like there was something stuck in its lungs. I brought you some donuts, I said. Can I bring them in? I knew it was too much to ask, so soon, but I couldn't help it. The shut-in was silent. I waited. It waited with me.

Is it okay if I come here sometimes? I said finally. Like this? To talk?

Tap, the shut-in went. Tap-tap.

. . .

I went to class. The teacher said Essays are due today. I looked down at my desk. I didn't remember anything about a paper, how long it was supposed to be, what it was supposed to be about. I pulled some notes out of my notebook, clipped them together, and passed them to the front. My heart was racing and I rubbed my chest, sweating. Transparencies flashed on the overhead projector, full of thick black lines, and neither the lines nor the words the teacher said about them made any sense. I pulled my sleeves over my hands, put the dirty hems to my mouth, breathed. It's funny how some spaces make you feel terror and others make you feel safe. That classroom got to me. Sometimes my own house got to me. But the shut-in couldn't leave its house, could it? No matter what it felt. Or, it could, but it didn't. So it must feel safe, in that case. Maybe it was the only place it felt safe and that's why it didn't leave. I watched the projector. I breathed through my sleeves. Then the hour was over and everyone jumped up as if, like me, they couldn't wait to leave. I hurried with them; that felt good. No one was paying any attention to me, no one was thinking Oh, that person is doing something we aren't doing. I was part of the mass funneling through the doorway, someone's bag stroking my shoulder, someone else's shoelaces tapping my foot. We squeezed through the door and then fanned out and out until the mass thinned and I was alone again. I stopped in front of a vending machine and felt in my pocket for change. I got a Twix. It was so loud in the halls. Sometimes it seemed like everyone was talking at once. Schools are like that. They make you think the wrong things; most people are probably not talking at any given moment. There is probably more silence than anything else in the world. And yet you'd think, in this school, no, everyone is talking, everyone is going somewhere, the mass goes on and on.

I went straight to the shut-in and sat by the door, legs crossed on a mat so old and dirty it was almost a part of the concrete. The package of donuts was gone. I took a Twix out of its wrapper. The shut-in stepped, stopped, breathed. Knowing I was there. I was part of a mass today, I said. The shut-in was quiet. I didn't say anything about forgetting to write the paper. Or about what I'd thought about rooms. I finished the chocolate, savoring each bite. The sky got darker in steps, as if the sun were walking down a staircase. I watched my knees change color. When they were black I stood up. The shut-in hadn't moved. And I was filled, for the second time that day, with wonder.

I wrote to it every day. *There's something wrong with me, too. You can't see with my clothes on. I wouldn't show you. I mean, because it's private. But I could tell you about it. If you wanted to know. It's very rare. I am very rare.*

What was it missing? An arm? An eye? Part of its face? Perhaps it had been burned, deformed, broken up in some way. Its possible beauty didn't occur to me. I don't think there are any beautiful people who stay inside all day. If you stop seeing other people, you stop knowing what makes people think you look nice or not. You have to know: Are people looking at me, or away? And if they look at me, what does that look mean? I wondered if the shut-in ever thought about what I was like. Maybe I was attractive, in a way that other people hadn't noticed before. Maybe my voice was soothing, what I said interesting. Maybe my handwriting was intelligent. If you didn't think it was at least possible to be liked, you would never look anyone in the face, you would never pick up the phone, you would never leave your house. I had thought for a long time that I was just waiting for something to happen to me, and that that was the point of living. To become a part of something else.

We could talk about moms and dads. But it had been a long time since I had had parents; and it must have been the same for the shut-in, nothing I'd seen or heard suggested parents, and so why bring them up? Inevitably the question would be: What did they think of you? I know what my parents thought of me. Revulsion is a huge feeling. And when it is directed at you, many moments in a row, it is exhausting. We could talk about being exhausted. You would think the shut-in would sound tired when it moved across the floor, but it never seemed that way. There was the energy of a question in its step, the flowing upward or outward toward something, an expectation. I think that was what excited me most: the sense of our energies meeting somewhere through the door, just beyond us. The way two hands feel before they touch. When you aren't touched a lot you can feel the closeness of things very acutely. And I felt this thing more than I thought I had ever felt anything in my life.

What about loving something? Have you ever done that?

I went to school the next day but didn't go to class. I sat instead in the lounge with a little bag of chips, trying to imagine that people were moving in fast-forward, like in time-lapse videos, where everything blurs together. The mass came to me, moved through me, around me, past me. You could do nothing. You could do anything. I ate one chip every five minutes and when the bag was empty I left.

The shut-in's front door was splitting, just like mine across the street. I often rubbed my palm against it, feeling how flimsy it was, with these long pieces peeling up from the bottom. Anyone could come in, I thought. If they really wanted to.

Do you think you could come to the window? I said, my lips almost on the wood. Could you? So I can see?

I heard it shift its weight, then pause. I paused, too, wondering if I had gone too far. Then it moved, receding, disappearing—and I stepped off the porch and into the dirt beneath the picture window, skinning behind the dead hedge. I put my fingers against the crumbling frame and stood on tiptoe to look and there was nothing for a while, just shadow, and then—a shape, a face, something terrible, a monster edging into view from behind the heavy curtains. I jerked back, mouth open, before realizing it was a mask I was looking at, not the shut-in's face. A pig mask, red-cheeked and grinning, snout pressed against the milky glass. I put my hand up to it. Was the shut-in old? Young? It was impossible to tell. But maybe not young. It seemed like something that had been around for a long time; there was something fixed about it, the way ghosts or trees or signs are fixed, to a certain place, and other things grow around them.

Hi, I said, scratching the glass like I would a dog's belly. Hi, hi.

It just looked at me. I felt how naked my face was, how it clung to my skull. Did it like how I looked? How well could it even see me, through the tiny holes in the mask, the dirty glass? Did it care? The shut-in turned its head to the side, slow, deliberate, like it was listening to something far away. All I heard were cars on distant roads, a sprinkler, someone yelling at a dog. Finally the mask turned back to me, as if to say Yes, we are alone. Hi, I said again, smiling. Hi, I see you, and it cocked its head, one pig-ear folded. I tried not to make my face do anything, to just let it be, and eventually it relaxed, loosening, floating, until I forgot what *face* even meant. And there was that sense again, of wonder, of how the shut-in's curiosity and my curiosity were rising to meet each other, its focus entirely on me, as mine was on it. And we were just bathing in that feeling and letting it build, the possibilities, until eventually I felt a sort of lessening, like we'd got full of each other, and so I smiled and said into the window Thank you, thank you, I'll come later, goodbye, and it put its own hand—stuck in a pilled gray glove—up to meet mine, and pressed.

When were you the most happy? Or are you happiest right now?

I took the nine o'clock bus to school. I held my backpack on my lap, my chin grazing the top strap. Someone came on and I waited for them to pass but they didn't; they stopped, they sat down. I moved as far as I could against the window. I could feel them looking at me, at the top of my head. Smiling, maybe. I felt shorter than everyone else, even though I am a normal size, because I never looked up when someone was staring. Hey, the person said. You go to Riverside, right? I didn't say anything. I hadn't said anything since I moved here, except when I talked to the shut-in. I could pretend that was my disease. Not being able to speak. Or to hear. Or to see. I squeezed my backpack, the corner of a notebook digging into my arm. I think we have a class together, the person said. I thought of sitting on the shut-in's step. Telling it about this moment. Someone talked to me, I would say. Looked at me in that way. Do you know what I mean? The way a person looks at you sometimes, wanting to know what you are. I felt the energy from the stranger's body overlapping mine, a black wave eating a lighter one, though the person didn't touch me. The bus stopped. The person waited for me to stand when they stood; I stayed still. I was an insect, bent completely over my backpack, breathing into its thick mesh. The stranger went; I stayed. I rode the bus home. The mass I had been a part of was broken; I had been cut off. That was okay. I had never really belonged to it, or even understood what it was.

I knew the shut-in was there even before I knocked. How did it know when I was coming? Maybe it didn't have to guess or watch; maybe it knew when I would come before I did. There was a sort of field between us now, electric, psychic. I want to come inside, I thought, closing my eyes, and then I said it aloud, my hands against the screen: I want to come inside.

Tap. Tap-tap.

But I didn't go in then, or the next day, or the day after that. I didn't go anywhere. I could feel the shut-in waiting, ready for me. Our windows facing each other. Things were even more quiet at home than usual and the house seemed softer, bigger; nothing pressed in on me, no assignments to do, no buses to take. I ate what I had in the cupboards, stayed on the couch, didn't even turn the TV on. I thought, I need to make myself really small. So I could fit in there, with it, when the time came.

My phone rang. The sound was so loud it made me flinch; no one had knocked on my door before, no one had ever called. Who could it be? The shut-in? Was I in the phone book? Was it? I answered on the eighth ring. Hello? I said, and even I knew I sounded wrong, scared, too quiet. So I said it louder. Hello? Hello! A voice asked for someone I'd never heard of; I almost laughed. No, I said, and now I was talking as loud as I ever wanted to: Who is this? The caller hung up but I stayed on the line. *You?* I whispered. *Is it you?*

I got my grades in the mail. Unlike in high school there was no judgment, no concerned note, no demand for a meeting to discuss my failures; just zeroes lined up in the credits column. I could take other courses next semester, or repeat the same ones; as long as I kept paying I could do what I wanted. What did I want? I stood there with the letter in my hands and looked out the window. For the first time, the shut-in's light was on, a dim white frost on the steps.

I brushed my teeth and put on clean jeans and a button-down shirt and combed my hair back into a ponytail before pulling the hood of my sweatshirt up. I did it in the dark; I didn't want it to see me getting ready, in case it was watching. Was I beautiful? I wondered. How could I be?

The night was warm, quiet, still; I took a deep breath and crossed the street, went up the steps. There was a mask on the mat, identical to the one it had worn in the window but smaller, child-sized. Snout facing out. I put it on. Reek of rubber. A new darkness. The door was open behind the screen and I felt my way through the gap, the air cooler over the threshold, heavier. The lock caught behind me. I blinked; the room was lit only by the porch light coming through the curtains and the mask forced me to take everything in in pieces: window, wall, wall, hallway. No furniture. A rugless floor. I could barely breathe. *Where are you*, I thought, and then I saw it: the shut-in, standing in the doorway to the kitchen. Its mask was so much bigger than mine, its round cheeks enormous, the smiling snout tipped in my direction. I stared. The shut-in's body was thick, the chest flat, wide, the heavy legs bowed, so the thighs didn't touch. It had the gloves on, socks pulled over the cuffs of its pants, the hood pulled tight around the mask, no inch of skin exposed. I still could not see what was wrong with it. I moved closer, so close I could easily touch any part of it if I wanted to. I was sweating. Giddy with something. I smiled. It mirrored me, head cocked. Arms hanging at its sides. *Well?* it seemed to be saying. Well, well, here we are. I said that, out loud: Here we are. My voice muffled inside the mask. All these things between us—masks, eyes, screen doors, windows, houses—filter after filter after filter. I could hear its harsh breath, as loud as mine. I came closer. I could see the eyes, deep behind the rubber holes, so featureless—just eyes, not even a color or a shape beyond the round pig-shape, black in the middle and something else all around and then white and then, presumably, skin, hair, a nose, a mouth—or nothing, maybe there was nothing—and it was trying to tell me something, I thought: That it understood me? That this was it? Or that this was just the beginning? Our masks almost touched, the snouts wavering at different heights, only very slightly mismatched.

Then its hand met mine and the moment crazed in all directions, like a crack in tempered glass, moving faster than I could follow. I gripped its fingers, feeling the shape of them beneath the rough glove. This is you, I said. It nodded like *Yes*, like we were ordinary people in a room, like it didn't matter if we could see each other, if the masks were on or off, because it was more than the mask or whatever could be beneath, and so it could leave it on, it could stay as it was, indefinitely, not showing itself, because I had already seen it, hadn't I? Hadn't I seen everything? It had invited me in. It had touched me. It had listened and existed and that, the shut-in said with its eyes, with its gloved hand, was enough. But the shut-in was wrong. It wasn't enough, because I wanted to know what was under there, still, beneath that mask, the gloves, the clothes, and I was free, in the world, to do what I wanted, I was not bound to these four walls like it was, and that was the difference between us: I was still in the world, just barely, and so with both hands I gripped the sides of its mask and pulled, hard, snapping the elastic that held the mask in place, the shut-in's head wrenched forward, enormous, exposed, and the sound it made was terrible, not a human sound at all, much more like an animal, which is what it turned out I was—the shut-in had trusted me, and I had trusted myself, but never again.

RAG

IT WAS wet inside her mouth, on the long slide down her throat. Embraced on all sides. Breathed in. I'd never been touched like that, so totally, total darkness. I got her to the end, of air, of feeling, of a body, of will. Of herself. What a struggle! Just to breathe, to do just once more what she'd done her whole life: exist. It was a shock, the simplicity of it, how I could so profoundly interfere with this creature, who, with all her skills and talents and graces, could not triumph over a mere scrap of trash. I triumphed over him, too, in the end, the one who put me there in the first place, who thought I was only his tool. She'd thought that, too. They were right in most ways. Not all.

. . .

I didn't really know what it meant. What it means. What do I mean? It's a hand that gives me meaning, and yet, I do know some things. I know what it means to be soft, to be limp, to glide along a slick surface, to gather, to suck, to twist, to soak, to lie still. To become something suddenly very hard, immovable, in the body of the beloved. To transform. My nature. I don't judge his, or hers. I turned him into a murderer, her into a corpse. Or maybe I only brought what was already in them into being. As willingly as I had done everything else.

I had touched that whole house while in her hands. Every inch of wood, of glass, of stone. She reached for me again and again. I rose to the occasion. After she was done for the day he took me and wrapped me around himself, grunted and spilled. Such a delight, to be manipulated by them. My beloveds. Sped further along the path of my undoing, every hour becoming softer and softer, thinner, more sensitive, wiser. Though I was washed in the hottest water the stains remained, hers and his: polish and semen, oil and dust. Folded. Unfolded.

We all want to get inside. Maybe your way isn't really any good at all. You can only go so far. I can fit into most holes. I can't break. Can't crack. And what of them? Their bodies? How they did it, what they did? How they dissolved. Her hair, her eyes, the way her arms lay on the floor when I was through. The split corners of her mouth. His bloody knuckles. Don't look. Consider, instead, the thing that came between them, that brought them together: Humble, happy rag. Sad rag. Used, bleached, spoiled, rinsed, dormant. Good for restoring things to beauty, to cleanliness, to a shine. Absorbing dirt, lust, so much of what is living. Absorbing life itself.

Certainly there is a history of the incident, going back before my time: injuries, a childhood illness, ostracism, mental disorder, loneliness, screams. A history of chance. These things I can't know; they don't really touch me. But what about love? What about fascination, with the simplest, most mundane things. Domestic things. Women's things. The household, the home, something helpful, helpless, a chore, women's work—a servant of a servant. He didn't know how to use me as she did; he was clumsy when he tried. He left streaks. He had to use me for his own purposes, to be a man, to invent violence out of something previously purely innocent. Out of one small thing, a romance. Who uses, who is used? His desire, her desire—they aren't mine. But I borrowed them. Faithful. Faithless.

There was a moment when he could have taken me out of her throat, or at least not stuffed me in so far, but he needed to cross the line. I helped him, I admit—so docile, so well suited for the task. He left me inside her; that is where they found me, distending that narrow passage. Covered in their cells. He'd held me with his bare hands and that was where he made his mistake. When I was free again, plucked back into the light and asked to speak, I spoke. First her undoing, then his. Every object conspires against man, is used and then uses.

What did you do? they asked. What did *you* do? I answered.

He is no longer able to do anything more than imagine a woman, to hold her in his mind for a moment before letting her go. That's not so bad, is it? He must let all of them go, now. How successful I was, doing my small jobs. How I saved you all a lot of grief.

ACKNOWLEDGMENTS

Thanks to Danielle Meijer, Emily Bell, Meredith Kaffel Simonoff, H. Peter Steeves, Javier Ramirez, Kathe Koja, Kenny Childers, Na Kim, Jackson Howard, Naomi Huffman, and the Corporation of Yaddo.

And to William Nickell, Charlotte Rae, and Bonnie, all my love.